OUR MISSING Colored

Quashon Davis

Publisher's note: This is a work of fiction. Any resemblance to actual persons (living or dead) or references to real people, events, songs, business establishments or locales is purely coincidental. All characters are fictional, and all events are imaginative.

For my brother, Jamil Gilmer. I can only hope to positively impact this world as much as you did. Until I can make you laugh again, rest easy.

Thank you, Kisha Green for everything,

Just past downtown Newark, New Jersey, on a usually quiet end of Passaic Avenue, sits Topps Diner. It's a staple of the state that has been serving thousands of customers a week since 1942. The small black and white building is one of the most popular spots for people to hit after a night out, and tonight is no different. For Alex and Tamica, this is the last stop on their first date. After a movie and drinks at a lounge, they're both ready to eat. Alex is a young web developer, and Tamica works at the mall. He's having a good time, but he's frugal with his money and Tamica clearly hasn't been out with too many men that had any. At the movie she ordered popcorn, candy, soda, chicken tenders, and nachos. At the lounge she ordered five drinks. Even though he was ready to call it a night after the lounge, she told him she was hungry, and well, he's a nice guy. After a twenty- minute wait, they're finally seated at a booth with a view of the streetlight on the corner.

"Hi folks, my name is Deirdre and I'll be your server today. Can I start you off with something to drink?" she asks.

"I'll have water for now," says Alex.

"Um…. can I have a Vodka and Cranberry?" Tamica asked their server with a slight attitude.

"Of course. I'll be right back with your drinks," Deirdre says before walking off.

Alex tried to hide his annoyance, but it was hard. He'd calculated all the money he'd spent and was not happy about it. Thirty for the movie, forty for snacks at the movie, and another forty for drinks at the lounge. After the fifty the diner is about to cost him, he'll be out at least a hundred and fifty bucks. Maybe if he concentrated on her a little more, he'd forget about the money he's spent.

"So, you said you work in the mall. What mall are you at? What store do you work in?" he asks.

"I'm in Livingston Mall. I work at Foot Locker," Tamica responded.

"That's cool. I used to collect sneakers,"

"Oh yeah? Why'd you give it up?" Tamica asked.

"I grew out of it. After college, I got my job and realized that it just wasn't a smart investment every month,"

"You went to college? Nice. I knew you were smart. When you came up to me in the club I told my girl, Zia *'I think he's smart girl.'*

"I see. Yeah, I went to Rutgers New Brunswick. I guess I am smart. What about you? Are you in school?" he asks.

"School? Naw, I don't have time for that," she answered.

"Oh really? What do you do besides work at the mall?" he asked.

"I'm tryin' to get this money,"

"Um… how exactly?"

"I do a few things. I do hair, drive Uber sometimes, and I babysit,"

"What's your ultimate goal though? What do you want to do?" he asked.

"Well, I'm hoping to make manager at Foot Locker. Once that happens, I can stop ubering and babysitting. Eventually, I'll get Saturdays off.

Alex stared at her in disbelief. He just realized that the whole evening was a waste of time and money. Tamica looked really good, but she had no long- term goals and he's all about education and growth. He sat and forced smiles while she ordered another drink, appetizers, and dessert after her main course.

"I had a really good time. I can't wait to do this again," Tamica said as he opened the car door for her.

"Me neither," he lied with a big smile.

As soon as he closed her door, his smile changed to a frown as he walked around to his car door to get in. The car sped toward 280 west. As they got closer to the East Orange exit, Tamica was almost home.

"Do you want to come in for a little while?" she asked seductively.

"You live alone?"

"No, but my mother don't care. We just gotta be quiet," she laughs.

"That sounds tempting. I don't think…"

Before he can respond, police lights come up behind him.

"Here we go with the bull," he says.

Alex pulled over and shut his car off. Before the officer got out of his car, Alex quickly took out his license, registration and insurance card. He angrily rolled down the window and waited.

"These cops are so annoying," Tamica said loudly.

"Don't make it worse," Alex whispered.

They hear the cop's door open and close, and he walks up slowly.

"Good evening. License, registration, and insurance please," he requested in a low but firm voice.

Alex handed the officer his paperwork and tried to hide his annoyance.

"Is this your car?" asks the officer.
"Yes sir," Alex responds.

"Okay. Give me a minute. I'll be right back," the officer says walking back to his car.

"This is ridiculous. We didn't even do anything," Tamica says.

Alex doesn't say anything. He hates cops and the situation isn't sitting well with him. He wasn't speeding or breaking any laws. The fact that they always harass him is annoying.

"I know it's because I drive a Lexus. These cops hate brothas," he says.

"But the cop is black," Tamica mumbled.

"Is he? I couldn't even tell," Alex questions.

"Actually, I'm guessing. I'm not sure. He sounded black,"

Before they could get their thoughts together, they once again hear the car door open and close. He walked up to the window and handed Alex his paperwork back.

"Can you step out of the car for me please?" The officer asked.

The light he's shining in their faces is so bright that they can't see anything.

"Why do I hafta get out the car? I didn't do anything," Alex protests.

"Sir, I need you to step out of the car for me," the cop tells him calmly.

Alex opened his car door and stepped out of the car. His eyes were trying to re-adjust after having the bright light in them. The cop guided him to the side of the car where he puts his hands up against it forcefully

"Can you just tell me what I did wrong?" he asks.

As his eyes finally start to focus, Alex looks down and sees a pair of white Air Force Ones on the cops' feet. Confused, he looks over to see a Toyota Camry with a police light on top of it.

"What the hell?!" Alex says

Before Alex can comprehend what's going on, he gets hit over the side of the head with a baton. He falls unconscious and Tamica began to scream. The 'cop' presses a tissue over her nose and mouth with a substance that knocks her out. He puts her in his car and speeds away, leaving Alex lying in the street.

CHAPTER ONE

There's a Real Problem

The police car pulled up to East Orange General Hospital. Two officers stepped out of the car: a short older white man, and a very young tall black woman. They head inside and get into the old rickety elevator.

"You know the deal rook; when we get to him, I'll do all the talking," the older guy said with arrogance in his voice.

"Yes sir," she replied sarcastically.

They get a nurse to tell them where to go, and head to room 520. When they walk in, the doctor has just finished stitching up Alex's head.

"Mr. Boylen, I'm Officer Mills, and she's Officer Merrit. We want to ask you some questions about what happened while it's still fresh in your mind, if you feel up to it," says the short old white guy.

His uniform is immaculate, with a duty belt full of attachments. Ray Mills is an old school white cop that works in a predominantly black neighborhood. He typically believes in 'guilty until proven innocent.' With only 3 years until he retires, Mills doesn't believe in working hard. He's all about shortcuts and closing cases as easily as he can. Nowadays his snacks and the fish place he owns in the suburbs are much more important than the job.

"No problem. Call me Alex," he said as he sat on the hospital bed.

"Alex, can you tell us exactly what happened?" Mills asks.

"Sure, I was on a date with a woman. Her name is uh, Tamica. I was taking her home and I saw the police lights behind me, so I pulled over. He shined a bright light in my face, and I couldn't see. He told me to step out of the car, so I did. That's when I noticed he had sneakers on. When I looked at his car, I noticed it wasn't a police car. That's when he hit me with something. I must've passed out," says Alex.

"Did you see what kind of car it was?" asks Mills.

"It was a Camry, black I think," Alex says.

"Did you get a look at the guy at all?" Mills asks.

"No. After he shined that bright light in my eyes, I couldn't see anything. By the time my eyes finally focused again, he knocked me out."

"I appreciate this. We'll be in touch with you soon," says Mills.

"Wait a minute, officers, what happened to Tamica? Is she okay?" asks Alex.

"Well Alex, unfortunately it looks like she's missing. She wasn't at the scene and there were signs of a struggle," Mills says.

"What? My God…" Alex says while putting his hands to his mouth.

"I'm very sorry. We'll be in touch," Mills concluded before exiting the room.

Before they reached the elevator, Mills already knew what his young partner was thinking.

"Merrit, before you give me your opinion that I didn't ask for, just know this is an isolated incident. It's probably her ex-boyfriend or someone that had it out for this woman. It's not part of some conspiracy," Mills informed.

"The girl worked at the mall: I doubt if she had someone that had it out for her enough to impersonate a cop," she replied.

"So, what are you saying Merrit?"

"I'm saying that women have been disappearing for months and nothing is being done about it,"

"This again? Come on, that's a rumor. We're not flooded with reports of missing women,"

"Of course, we're not. It's not a priority," she stated.

"Here we go. You pulling the race card again, rook?"

"It's not about pulling a card. We're gonna investigate the scene and talk to a couple of her friends and family members. After that, she just becomes another missing girl," she says.

"Merrit, I like you. I really do. You've got a lot of energy. You want to do the right thing. When I was your age, I wanted to fix all the wrongs in the world also. You're twenty years old. You've been a cop for a few months. We're band-aids kid. We're here to silence all the bad stuff long enough for everyone to get a good night's sleep. I realized a long time ago that I couldn't change the world. Drugs? You could spend your whole career getting them off the street. Guess what? They'll keep coming in, the dealers will keep distributing them, and people will keep getting high."

"Are you saying that we might as well not exist?" Merrit asked.

"Not at all. I'm saying that worrying about the things that are right in front of us will make you successful at this job. It's not always a conspiracy. I'm gonna retire soon, and when I do, you can chase after every conspiracy you want. Until then, we're gonna just follow the leads we get, and handle the crimes we see," says Mills.

"Whatever," she murmured.

"Listen, I get it. I read your file. I know it's not easy. I know who your father was,"

"That's not fair. Me wanting to find missing women has nothing to do with who my dad was. I never met him. I have eyes Mills. I see women missing. It's increasing every day. There's something going on,"

"Well, I respectfully disagree with you, rook. We're not detectives. And you're from New York, right? Why didn't you just join the NYPD? Even I remember how famous your dad was over there,"

"That's why I came over here. I didn't want any special treatment because my father was a cop,"

"What about your mom? Is she still in New York?" asks Mills.

"I don't know who my mother is. I grew up in the system,"

"I'm sorry. I didn't know,"

"You did know Mills. You read my file,"

"I didn't read all of it,"

"Whatever. Tell me what else you didn't read,"

"Well, your file said you were rich. How can you be rich if you grew up in the system? You got a juvee record too. Actually, you got quite the juvee record. I didn't understand any of it,"

"You could've just asked me,"

"I didn't wanna be nosey Merrit,"

"You didn't want to be nosey, so you just read my file? You're all heart Mills. I don't know where I came from or who my mother was. I grew up in the system. When I was old enough, I tried Ancestry.com, but it only told me about my fathers' side. It was like my mother and her entire family history never existed,"

"But don't you have a brother?"

"J.J. isn't my real brother. When I found out who my father was, his best friend was Jay Jones,"

"Jay Jones, the God of Manhattan? He's the greatest Knick of all time,"

"Yeah well, when he found out who my dad was, he reached out to me. He took me in. His son James is like a brother, and he's just Uncle Jay,"

"But isn't his son a singer?" Mills probed.

"Yeah,"

"But why do you…"

"Mills, you ask too many Goddamn questions," fussed Merrit.

"I'm your senior training officer. I can ask anything I want,"

"I don't work for you. I work for the city: my city," she said.

"Your city, Merrit? You're from New York. I've worked in East Orange for 30 years. I know this city better than most people,"

"Yeah? Where do you get the best chicken wings? How about the best soul food? Where's the best barber? You worked here for 30 years, and you don't know shit,"

"Even though I don't like talking to you, I know the answers to those. Prospect has the best chicken wings," says Mills

"No, Springdale ave," she replies.

"Best Soul Food is the old Diner,"

"The place that's in the old diner is trash. The best soul food is in the Muslim section on 4th Avenue," she says.

"Anybody ever tell you that you got a bad attitude?" asks Mills.

"Nobody I give a damn about,"

"You're all heart Merrit. You're all heart,"

When they get back to the station, Merrit headed to her desk and started cleaning it off. She was ready to get that uniform off and forget about the job for a little while. It'd been a tough first few months for her on the force. She'd fought her way through the academy, while *'the old boys club'* tried to keep her from succeeding. But Kora Merrit was too tough. She'd outperformed the male recruits throughout the academy. Her toughness and intelligence couldn't be questioned, but her attitude was a different matter. Maybe it was bitterness from growing up in foster homes, maybe it's from fighting everyday as a kid, but whatever it is, her attitude rubs the other cops the wrong way. The veterans don't think rookies should have any type of attitude; they should just be quiet yes-men and women that do whatever they're told, but Kora isn't that type at all. She's rugged and honest and doesn't give a damn what anyone thinks. Standing at five foot eleven, she's tried to scale back her feisty mentality since joining the force. As she finishes straightening up her desk and getting ready to head out, Mills walks by her desk.

"Where you goin rook?" he asks

"I'm gettin outta here. It's quittin' time," she said.

"Not for you, rook. You gotta type up the paperwork on the incident we just got back from,"

"Are you kidding Mills?"

"Nope. Maybe you'll be on the force long enough to have a rook partner one day, which I doubt. If you do, you can make them type up all the paperwork. I gotta get to my card game. Have a good night,"

Kora angrily started typing up the incident report. About ten feet in front of her desk, the doors to the precinct opened, and in walked an officer dragging a young black man. He looked all of nineteen, with tears streaming down his face. The officer was yelling directly into his ear.

"Walk!" The giant white officer shouted.

Although the terrified young man complied and tried to slowly walk, the aggressive officer began to drag him. Kora stood up, her first instinct was to go over there, but she took a second to think. Clearly, she should've taken longer than a second because she walked quickly over to the cop who was dragging the young man.

"Officer, why don't you let me take him?" she offered.

"Excuse me?" he replied.

"I'm just finishing up some paperwork. I can book him so you can get outta here," she offered again.

He stared at her for a few seconds before he responded.

"Why would you do that?" he asked.

"I need all the practice I can get," Kora said.

"Fine, take him. It's quitting time anyway. I can't wait to get outta here,"

He pushed the suspect over to Kora and began to turn and walk.

"Oh wait, officer, what's the charge? Kora asked.

"Resisting arrest," the officer responded.

"Okay, but what was he under arrest for?"

"He smelled like marijuana. I told him he was under arrest, and he got aggressive with me, so here we are," he stated.

"Okay, did you find any marijuana on him? I'll book it into evidence," she says with a straight face.

"No, I didn't. Resisting arrest is good enough to get him into the county for a few days," he shot back feeling irritated at her questions.

"How do you figure that?" Kora asked.

"He'll get arraigned tomorrow. His bail will be maybe a thousand. He doesn't have it. He'll hafta stay in the county jail for a while. Good night," the cop said, walking away.

Kora led the young man to her desk and sat him down. He's still crying. She takes a tissue and wipes his face before getting back on her computer.

"What's your name?" she asks.

"Nii," he responds.

"Okay, is that short for anything?"

"No ma'am," he responded.

"Okay, tell me what happened,"

"I was walking home from the store and this cop pulled over and asked me where I was hiding the weed. I told him I don't smoke. He went through my book bag, my pockets; he even pulled my pants down. When he didn't find anything, I told him I just wanted to go home. He said he was arresting me because he could tell I had been smoking, and I had to have weed on me somewhere. When I started crying, he told me I was resisting,"

"That's it? That's the whole story?" Kora questioned sounding skeptical.

"Yes ma'am," he replied.

The van to take the nightly detainees to the county jail is leaving in fifteen minutes. Kora knew she didn't have much time. She sighed deeply while quickly dialing a number on her cell phone.

"What's your last name?" she asked the scared young man in front of her.

"Otellan," he replies.

"Geez, where are you from?"

"I am from…"

Kora held up one finger as she began her phone call.

"Hi there. It's Kora Merrit," she said.

"Oh hell. What do you want this time?" the voice on the other end asked.

"I need a favor," Kora says.
"Of course, you need a favor. Didn't I tell you not to call me?" the voice on the other end questions sounding more irritated by the second.

"Don't be like that. You said when I met you that you knew my dad, and if I ever needed anything to just call,"

"I said I met your dad. He and I played basketball thirty years ago together. I played in a league on west 4th street with him. We hung out a few times, that's all!"

"Well, I never even got to meet my dad. He died before I was born you know. And for the record, you gave me your cell number when we met.

"You make me sick. What do you want rookie?"

"You too with this rookie shit? It's gettin' a little old," she responded sounding pissed.

"You know, only you would call the mayor of East Orange and curse like you're talkin to one of your friends," he said.

"We are friends, Ned. When we met at the Christmas Party and you said you knew my dad, you said…"

"Okay okay! What do you need?" he asked loudly.

"There's a kid here, Nii Otellan, he was picked up for marijuana and resisting arrest. It was all bullshit, and they're about to transfer him to the county,"

"Fine, done. And don't be calling me for shit like this," he responded.

"Don't be like that, Mayor Brown," Kora said with a snicker.

"You make me sick," he growled before hanging up.

New York City.

In the heart of Times Square there's a legendary basement music club called the Iridium. Known for its jazz, tonight they featured a talented R & B singer that goes by the name J.J. Crisp. His smooth voice and talent on the piano set him apart from a lot of artists. J.J. doesn't perform a lot, he writes music for other artists and he's not in it for the fame. People love him though, and whenever he does perform it sells out quickly. After a standing ovation, he is led back to his dressing room. A short woman with a clipboard opens the door for him and smiles.

"That was a great show. You're so talented," she complimented.

"I appreciate that. What's your name? J. J. asks.

"Me? Oh, I'm Stephanie," she says fully cheesing.

"Nice to meet you Stephanie,"

"Oh…I…thanks…um…could we?" she tries to ask while holding her phone up.

"Of course," he says, grabbing her tightly and taking a selfie.

"Oh my God! Thank you J.J.," Stephanie says, closing his door and running off.

The tall crooner sits down in front of the mirror and stares at himself with a big frown. A tear rolls down his cheek, then another. He picks up his phone and looks over his missed text messages. He sees one from Kora:

"Big bro. Drinks tonight please! Our spot in 90,"

A smile comes across his face. He was 20 years old when his Father took in Kora, who was sixteen. His Dad Jay, one of the greatest basketball players of all time, took her in as soon as it was discovered that her dad was his best friend Roger, who was killed before she was born. The two of them love each other like siblings. They talk almost every day. He looks forward to their talks more than his performances, groupies, even adventures.

J.J. walked out of the rear exit of the Iridium and got into his jet -black BMW I8. You could barely hear the hum of the engine as he sped toward the Lincoln Tunnel.

"Call dad," he said to the car.

"Hey son," his father, Jay, said with pride.

"Hey Pop. What you and mom up to?"

"Well, your mom is watching Property Brothers. I'm just sitting here waiting for her to doze off, so I can change the channel,"

"I know that's right. Tell Mom I said hey," J.J. requested.

"Your son is saying hi to you Shel," his father said into the background.

"Hi son! I know you killed it tonight," J.J. hears his mom say.

"Whatchu up to J.J.? Where you headed?" his dad asked.

"Meeting up with Kora to have a drink," he responded.

"Oh, cool. Make sure you kiss your sister for me," Jay said.

"I will Pop,"

"What's on your mind J.J.? You sound like something is bothering you,"

"Nothin' Pop. I'm just tired,"

"Work hard, play hard son. You know that," laughs Jay.
"You haven't worked in twenty years Pop,"

"Damn right. I worked hard as hell on that court when I did,"

"Do not tell me another story dad,"

"I don't do that all the time," Jay said sounding slightly offended.

"Yes, you do. I'll see you and Mom this weekend. You still having the barbeque?" J.J. asked.

"Yeah I am. Bring your own food. Nobody wants that healthy shit you eat," Jay said.

"Goodnight, Pop,"

"Later son,"

J.J. sat in traffic for almost an hour, just trying to get through the tunnel. It's a busy night as usual, with plenty of people shuffling in and out of the city. Speeding is therapeutic for J.J. Unfortunately, there was too much traffic tonight for him to do it. He finally worked his way through the tunnel and took the exit for Hoboken. After paying to park his car in a private lot, he made his way to one of the many bars on the Hoboken strip. The line to get in the bar stretched all the way around the block. J.J. pulled his hat down almost over his eyes and calmly walked past everyone until he got right up to the velvet ropes.

"You see that long line going all the way down the street, right?" the bouncer asked.

He lifted up his hat just enough for the bouncer to see his distinct, big, brown eyes.

"Oh! Whatsup bro? I didn't know that was you. Come on in," he says, opening the velvet ropes for J.J. to go inside.

"Yo, Rolisha, sit him at the table in the back behind the stage, and unscrew the light bulb," the bouncer instructs her.

J.J. slipped him a fifty and they quickly shared a bro-hug.

"Thanks bro," says J.J.

"You got it. Your sister coming too?" the bouncer asks.

"Yeah. She should be here any minute"

"Okay, I'll have her sent to your table when she gets here,"

"You da man bro," J.J. complimented.

He was sitting at his table in the back of the room behind the stage and the dance floor. The area was dark, and no one could see who he was. He people watched for a few minutes and ordered some drinks. It felt good to be in a crowded place and have no one recognize him. At six foot five, he stands out most of the time. Strangely enough, even though he's a successful singer/songwriter, most people consider him 'Jay's son.' He's tried hard to get out from under his dad's massive shadow. His dad, Jay, always hoped J.J. would follow in his footsteps and play pro basketball. J.J. liked playing, but not like he loved music. By high school, his world revolved around it. He played basketball his freshman year, then gave it up entirely. His dad was disappointed, but he understood. After a few more minutes, Kora comes walking up to the table. He jumps up excited and hugs her tightly.

"Hey little sis," he said, greeting her warmly.

"Hey. I'm so glad I got outta there. How are you J.J.?" she asked as they sit down.

"I'm good, I guess. Had a show tonight."

"Oh yeah? How did it go?"
"Pretty good. It was sold out. I did my thing,"

"Okay, then why do you look like you lost your best friend?" she questioned while looking at him closely.

"I don't know. I think it's just one of those days,"

"Yeah, well it must be going around then. I definitely had one of those days myself,"

"Oh yeah? Had to bust a lotta criminals today?" J.J. questioned

"Not really. Sometimes it feels like I work with the criminals,"

"You do sis," he laughed.

"My senior partner, Mills. I just want to introduce him to Sam Jackson so bad," she said with no humor in her voice.

"You always want to introduce someone to your Sam Jackson. You're so crazy,"

"It's not me J.J., it's all these crazy mofos out here,"

"Well, we don't hafta talk about work tonight sis. We just gotta get drunk," he teased.

J.J.; we both drove here. I can't afford to be drunk in public. They're probably watching me right now. It's gonna be Mountain Dew for me," answered Kora.

"You're paranoid sis. Don't let those 'good ole boys' get in your head. You made it, and it had nothing to do with who your father was,"

"Yeah, you're right about that."

"Trust me, Kora, having a father that everyone looks up to is overrated,"

"Why you say that?" she asked.

"I love dad, but so many doors open for me because of who he is. When I signed with Arena Records, the first thing they asked was could my dad come down and take some pictures. Every time I do an interview, they want to talk about my dad. Every time I sign autographs or take pictures, people ask how my dad is doing. I wonder if I would've made it without him," J.J. tells her as he refuses to make eye contact.

"You don't hafta wonder J.J., he is your dad. You should take advantage of that as much as you can. You'll never pay for a meal in the city, or to get into a spot. And how can you wonder if you woulda made it? You're selling out venues all over the city. Your dad is proud of you. At least you get to see the pride on his face when he talks about you. I never got to meet mine," Kora replied.

"I know sis. There could be worse situations than the one I'm in. I met your dad a couple of times, but I was too young to remember. My dad talks about him all the time. He really loved him. He told me the story about how he died a million times."

"Me too," Kora responded.

"He was a hero. He took down the world's deadliest assassin," they both say at the same time, while laughing and taking a swig of their drinks.

"Do you ever wonder though…?" J.J. started to ask but paused

"What?"

"Do you ever wonder who your mom was?" he asked.

"Yeah. It's whatever though. He had a wife, but they were separated. I'll never know, but hey: I got you, Uncle Jay, and Aunt Shel. I'm good, believe me,"

"Awww come on Kora! You're not good. You've been mad at the world since you got outta that last nasty group home. If you want to learn more about yourself, you should. Hell, I'm curious myself," J.J. said sounding serious.

"Naw, I'm good. It's like she never existed or something. I gave up on that years ago,"

"I understand that, but your dad was one of the best detectives that ever lived. I'm just sayin…"

"Drop it J.J. I got real crap to deal with," she snapped.

"Like what? Whatsup?" he asked.

"I don't want to get into that stuff. I just want to drink tonight,"

"All you drink is Mountain Dew!" J.J. reminded her and laughed out loud!

The two spent the next couple of hours drinking and eating bar appetizers. They both clearly needed it. For the first time in a couple of days, Kora genuinely laughed.

"Okay, I gotta get home. I got work in a few hours," Kora finally informed her brother.

"Yeah, yeah. How's Redd?" asked J.J.

"He's the same. I'm trying to distance myself from him. I could lose my job messing with that fool,"

"Yeah, okay. You've known that *'fool'* since you were ten years old. Ya'll need to just get married,"

"Redd is married to the streets. That's never gonna change. And I can't keep dealing with him now that I'm on the force. They'd love a reason to get rid of me, and it would be pretty easy to do while I'm still on probation."

"Yeah, but Redd would do anything for you,"

"I know he would, but he's a drug dealer, I'm a cop. And we're just friends. Okay, friends that hook up sometimes. But whatever, we cool. He got a girlfriend now anyway. I got too much goin on to worry about Redd," Kora told him sounding almost believable.

After a couple more hours, they said their goodbyes and headed their separate ways. J.J. took off for the tunnel, blasting music along the way. He fumbled through his pockets and pulled out a small amount of cocaine. As he tried to open the bag, the contents spilled on his hand. He quickly balanced the powder on his hand and sniffed it. He'd been using coke now for a couple of months. Depression was hitting him hard and he didn't know why. If you're on the outside looking in, J.J. had everything: his music was doing well, he was selling out small venues, the best in the business reached out to him to write their songs, and he's the son of one of the most famous athletes ever. Despite having all of that in his favor, J.J. just wasn't happy. He hid it from family and friends, always putting on a smile and cracking a joke, but on the inside, nothing was funny.

Kora didn't get to her apartment until 4:30am. By 4:33 she was in bed. Her phone started to ring before she could get comfortable. Rolling her eyes, she reached back out to her table.

"What Redd? It's after Four in the morning. She growled

"Whatsup Special K? What's goin on?" he asked.

"Whatchu want? Does your girl know you callin me this late?" Kora questions.

"Don't be like that. I just got off work.,"

"You're a drug dealer Redd. Don't talk like you're a regular guy."

"I'm a long shore-man Kora. Why you acting like that?"

"That's your night job. Don't play me Redd. You got a girl now. Shouldn't you be calling her at Four in the morning?"

"I got a girl now because you didn't want me to be your man," Redd countered.

"I didn't want you to be my man because you sell drugs. I'm a cop now, fool. I can't be in a relationship with a drug dealer. You know they watch me, right?"

"No doubt. I ain't mad atcha Special K, but you know you got mad love for me."

"Redd, I will hang up on you. What the hell do you want?"

"I just wanna see you, that's all," he answered.

"Redd, leave me alone. And I know you got drugs coming into the port. You're lucky I don't bust your ass."

"You can't bust me Special K. Come on now," he said, as he heard her hang up.

CHAPTER TWO

Unlikely Allies

Two days later, the squad car pulled up to the Shoprite on Main Street. There had been a big commotion in the parking lot, and a few other officers were there trying to calm everyone down.

"Great. What the hell is this all about?" Mills sighed.

They got out of the car and moved through the crowd toward the crime scene tape that is separating an old Chevy Blazer from the crowd. The officer standing in front of the tape was doing his best to keep everyone away from it.

"Hey. What happened here?" asked Mills.

"Looks like an abduction. Store owner said the woman that owns this truck was walking from the store, and when she got to her door, a couple of guys jumped out of a van parked next to her and snatched her," the officer informed.

Mills tried not to look at Kora, but he could feel her eyes burning a hole in his soul.

"Let me guess rook, this is part of your grand conspiracy where the big bad white man is trying to rid the world of the black woman? Give me a break,"

Instead of responding to him, she put on some gloves and began looking around the truck. There wasn't much to find; no broken glass or objects dropped onto the ground. She stood up frustrated and saw an officer holding a small child.

"Who's the little lady?" Kora asked, smiling and tapping the infant.

"She was strapped in the car-seat when her mom was taken," the officer told her.

"Do we know who the mother is?" asked Kora.

"Yes. Brandi Moorey, twenty-eight years old. She's a hairdresser in town. The child is hers, names Janiessa. There's no father listed on the birth certificate, and she has no grandparents or living relatives listed,"

"So, what's about to happen to this child?" she asks.

"She'll hafta be put into the system," the officer answered.

Kora watched as the officer placed the child in a baby-seat in one of the squad cars. She'd grown up in the foster care system and doesn't wish it on anyone. While staring at the small grinning infant, Kora drifts off to another place. The memories of her many group homes flood her mind, along with bad memories. Kora had to fight every day. She remembers the beatings, the fights, and the abusive foster parents that would take her and bring her right back after a few weeks.

"Wake up Rook," Mills said.

"Whatever. I guess you think this is a random abduction, right?" Kora asked.

"Of course, I do. It's a simple grab in a grocery store parking lot. This is what we call a *crime of opportunity*. That's all it is."

"Right," she responded.

"Well, come on Rook, let's get back to the station so we can punch out,"

"You go ahead Mills. I'm gonna walk back to the station."

"Yeah, okay. See you tomorrow," he responded, walking off.

Kora hung around for a while looking for clues, but there weren't any to find. After asking everyone if they'd seen anything, she walked out of the shopping plaza. Discouraged, the young officer heads down Main Street as the sun is slowly lowering on the horizon. She knows someone saw something, but the code of the street keeps everyone silent. As she walks past the park, Kora sees all the young weed dealers shooting a basketball. Without hesitation, she walked toward them. When they see her, they think about running off, until one of them says:

"You ain't gotta run fools, what she gonna catch all of us?"

They continue shooting the basketball while keeping an eye on Kora. She walked into the park and right up to the thin shirtless bandana clad young men.

"Hey fellas. Can I shoot?" she asked.

"I don't know, can you?" one of them asked sarcastically.

They laugh while one of them passes the ball to Kora. She makes a shot, then another, and another. The young men stare at her as she stands right outside of the three-point line and calmly makes shot after shot.

"Who the hell are you?" one of them asked.

"I'm just a cop. I ain't nobody special," she says, continuing to make shots.

"How the hell are you doing that?" one of the young dealers asked.

"My uncle taught me how to shoot. It's one of those things you never forget,"

"Damn girl!" Who's your uncle?!" he asked.

"You mean officer, right?" Kora asked.

"My bad, officer. No disrespect. Who yo uncle though?" he asked again.

"Jay Jones," she said.

"Get the hell outta here!" they all exclaim.

Kora took out her phone and pulled up a picture of her and Jay laughing and hugging at the Thanksgiving table. The young men tried to stay tough and emotionless, but the moment they see it, it's a big deal to them.

"Yo, that's crazy as hell!" one of them said.

"Why you a cop? You could just be chillin right now," the young man asks.

"I don't want to chill. I wanted to be a cop," Kora tells them proudly.

"That's whatsup ma…I mean officer! My bad," he says.

"You're good. What are your names?" she asks.

"Tito,"

"Rowe"

"Bit,"

"Will,"

"I'm Officer Merrit. I need some information," Kora requested.

"Hold up. You cool and all, but we ain't snitchin' on nobody," said Bit.

"I don't care about how you make your money. Black women, your women, are disappearing. Somebody's taking them. I want to put a stop to it. A woman was just grabbed over on Main Street in front of her baby. It's happening every week. I'm tired of it. It's not just here either. Now I know you got a code and even though it's to protect people doing illegal shit, I respect that. This woman grabbing shit though, I don't respect. It's some weak, cowardly bullshit. I hope you're with me on that. If you're not, then I'm good," she says, passing the basketball back to them.

"Naw, we with you Ma," Tito guarantees.

"Officer Merrit," she says.

"My bad officer. No disrespect. You right though. We ain't with that kidnapping shit," Tito says.

"Hell no. But we really don't know nothing officer," says Will.

"Just see if you can find out anything. You're in the streets 24-7; maybe you'll hear something. If you do, hit me up," Kora says, handing them her card.

"Aight Officer Merrit. We gotchu," Bit promises.

"Have a good day gentleman," she said, walking out of the park.

"Hey, Officer Merrit," Will called out to her.
"Yeah?" Kora turned back.

"What are you gonna do for us?" he asked.

"I'm gonna let you keep that pound of weed you got hidden in the trash can," she said while walking away.

The guys all laugh, impressed with Kora's skills.

After a few minutes, she makes it to the station. When she walks in, her captain is at the reception desk, picking up some papers.

"Why didn't you ride in with your partner, rook?" he questioned.

"I needed a little fresh air," she said.

"Is that right? You weren't trying to do police work without your partner were you?" he asked.

"No sir,"

"I hope not. Remember, you're not a detective. I hear you're good, but a hothead. Make sure you do the job you're paid to do and nothing else. The last thing you ever want to do is get on my radar, understand?"

"Yes sir," Kora answered with a straight face.

Before the captain is even out of sight, Kora makes a 'whatever' face and heads to her desk. She has no intention of changing anything.

Chapter Three

It's Always About Color

At a diner just outside the Lincoln Tunnel in Weehawken New jersey, Kora is enjoying happy hour with J.J. This is their routine whenever they can make it happen, but today they're waiting for one of their friends. Kora eats like a man; she has wings, nachos, spinach dip, and mozzarella sticks.

"How do you eat all that?" asked J.J.

"Don't judge me, okay? I'm stress eating," Kora responded.

"I thought we were gonna wait for Sean," he said.

"Sean's always late. J.J. I'm hungry,"

"You've got a point sis. That's actually true."

"I know. So, are you gonna talk about what's going on with you?" Kora questioned.

"Nothin's goin on with me sis.

"You know I'm a cop, right?" she asked.

"Come on Kora…"

"Don't come on Kora me, J.J. What are you on? And what are you depressed about?"

"I really don't know what you're…"

"Hey guys, I made it," says Sean.

He tried to kiss Kora on the cheek, but she lightly slapped his face away. He settles for a hug and shakes J.J.s hand before picking up the menu. Sean has been J.J.'s friend since middle school. A short chubby guy that's always smiling, Sean is an up-and-coming comedian with his first Netflix special dropping in a month.

"Why are you always late?" asked Kora.

"My fault. I was out here making this money," Sean answered still smiling.

"Oh God, please shut up," Kora teased.

"Why you always starting with me?" Sean asked.

"Because you make me sick! That's why I always gotta introduce you to my Sam Jackson," Kora laughs.

"What is your Sam Jackson," Sean asked eying her curiously.

"That's what she calls it when she has to curse someone out," J.J. informed his longtime friend.

"I like that. I might use that," Sean grins even wider.

"Well, I'm glad you made it. You better order before happy hour is over," J.J. said.

"I'll just pick from you guys. Kora always orders food for three people anyway. Greedy ass," Sean joked.

"Whatever. You eatin' my food though," Kora responded.

"Yeah, yeah. What's been goin on with you two though?" Sean asked.

"J.J. is going through something. He won't talk about it," Kora tells him.

"Oh yeah? Whatsup with you, bro? Sold out shows and artists hitting you up for beats got you down?" Sean teased.

"Shut up. I'm good. I have bad days like everybody else. You know how it is," J.J. said.

"You should take that medicine they got now for bad days," said Sean.

"What medicine?" J.J. asked and gives Sean the side eye.

"Booty," laughed Sean.

"Oh God. You're so stupid," Kora said, shaking her head.

Her phone begins to beep loudly. She looks at it and frowns.

"What's wrong?" asked Sean.

"I gotta go to work. Sorry guys, something big must've happened. It's an all-hands-on deck alert," she says, sliding out from the booth.

"It's all good. I'll just finish all this up for you," Sean said.

"I'll bet you will. J.J., I'll call you later." Laughed Kora.

As Kora sped up the turnpike-heading north. She tried to call Mills, but he didn't answer. She can't figure out what could be so important. In less than twenty-five minutes, she makes the trip to the precinct and quickly makes her way to the conference room. Everyone is sitting around confused. She asked one of the officers what's going on, but he just shrugged his shoulders. Everyone sits around for a few more minutes trying to figure out what's going on before the captain walked in.

"Okay everyone, let me have your attention please," the tall and annoyed captain said while heading up to the podium.

"At 5pm today, a seventeen-year-old young woman was abducted from a doctor's office on Central Avenue. The channel two news is on this, so of course, the mayor's office needs this young woman found quickly. We're gonna scour the city for the next eight hours, turn over every rock, hit up every informant you've

got. Her name is Vanessa Kirby. Put her picture up on the screen Riley," the captain requests.

'It's about time they started making missing sistas a priority up in here,' Kora thinks to herself.

Her and the other officers all stare at the screen waiting for the young woman's picture to show. After about ten seconds, the I.D. picture of the white woman takes up the entire length of the monitor. As the officers all look at the picture, Koras' blood is boiling. She just stares at the picture in disbelief, trying to understand if this is really what's happening.

"You ready to hit the streets rook?" asked Mills.

She doesn't respond, walking over to the captain instead.

"Can I have a word with you captain?" Kora asked.

He led her to his office and closed the door. The captain took a deep breath before sitting down.

"What do you want Merrit?" he asked, sounding annoyed already.

"In the few months that I've been here, I've seen cases of at least forty young black women who have been abducted. None of them have had a manhunt, or even gotten as far as a detective investigating them. When they're reported, the cops at the scene fill out a report and it goes into a file cabinet that no one uses. I've been complaining about this pattern of young black women being taken since I got here, and nothing's been done about it. Today I get called in on my off time, told it's all hands-on deck, a top priority, and you tell me it's because a white woman was taken?" Kora asked angrily.

"You have an issue following orders, rook?" he asked.

"No sir,"

"When you're in charge, you can prioritize things any way you want. Until that day comes, you have to follow orders. The orders today are to search for any leads regarding the disappearance of Vanessa Kirby. That's the only thing you should be thinking about. Are we clear?".

Kora stared at him angrily. Her lip was quivering. She wanted to give him the *'Sam Jackson treatment'* so bad! She thought hard about just cursing him out.

"Are we clear, rookie?" he asked again, a little more aggressively.

"Yes sir," she responded in a barely audible tone.

"I didn't hear you, rook," he said loudly.

"Yes sir," Kora said.

"Good. Now get the hell out of my office and do what you were instructed to do,"

Kora walked out and angrily sat at her desk. She watched as the other officers all scrambled around, getting organized before they hit the streets and searched for Vanessa Kirby. She can't believe that this is happening. Mills walked by and told her he'd be waiting for her in the parking lot. As she got up and grabbed her keys, she stopped and dialed her phone.
"Mayor Brown," a voice said.

"Hello Mr. Mayor. It's Kora Merrit," she said.

"Oh God. As if this day can't get any worse. You know when I gave you my card and said call if you ever need anything, I was just being nice right?"

"Don't be like that Mayor Brown. You knew my dad, remember?"

"Here we go. We played ball together, hung out once or twice! Do you know how busy I am today?"

"Well, I never got…"

"…To meet your father! I know!" he said loudly.

"What do you want this time?" he asked, trying to calm down.

"Black women are being taken every day all over the country. Right here in East Orange, young black women are disappearing weekly, with no investigation, no hoopla, nothing. This white girl gets snatched and the damn news is all over it. I need the same energy when our sistas disappear that this woman is getting," Kora responded.

"I understand. We cannot make it a color thing though. You know that. We have to treat kidnappings and abductions the same no matter who the victim is. The bottom line is, they're a victim, doesn't matter the color," the mayor said.

"It is about color. That's why we're sending the cavalry after this white woman. Why is she more important than any other black woman who has disappeared over the last month?" Kora blasts, banging her hand on the desk.

"You know I'm busy right? You're not gonna let this go until you hear something that satisfies you, are you?" he asked loosening his tie and feeling irritated.

"No, I'm not," Kora tells him flatly.

"Okay, okay. I tell you what. If we find Vanessa Kirby, I will start up a task force dedicated to dealing with the abductions of women in this city. I will personally recommend that you be in that task force. Is that fair?" he asked, trying to throw her a bone so Kora would back off.

"Yeah, that's fair,"

"Good. I have a press conference now. Can I go?" the mayor sarcastically requested

"Yes, you can. Thank you, Mr. Mayor," Kora responded

"Whatever,"

The mayor clicked off the phone and put it in his pocket while his wife fixed his tie. He stared into the mirror intensely.

"Was that the young rookie? The Merrit girl?" his wife asked.

"Yeah, why?" The mayor annoyingly responded.

"She reminds you of Hazel, doesn't she?" his wife asked.

"Yeah, a little," he admits with sadness in his eyes.

"I know she does. It's adorable seeing you interact with her. It reminds me of the way you and Hazel were,"

"Merrit gets on my damn nerves," the mayor says blowing out a frustrated breath.

"Sure, she does. Your daughter did as well. Take that young recruit under your wing. You need her as much as she needs you," his wife advised.

"I wouldn't go that far," he replied.

His wife cuts her eyes at him as she walks out the door.

Mills and Merrit drove through East Orange looking for Vanessa Kirby, or any signs of her. They, along with most of the other cops in the city, are all searching everywhere. After several hours of searching, the rain begins to fall over the city. It's looking like an impossible mission. One thing that's clearly annoying Kora is the tenacity with which Mills seems to be trying to find the woman. He seems almost desperate. Kora's not one to hold her tongue, but even she is attempting to show reserve. The young officer knows that if she gets into it with him over this, it's just going to end badly. She's watched for hours as he has circled blocks, shook down people on the street, asked businesses, and even tried calling his informants. She's aggravated and if she can just hold out for thirty more minutes, she won't get into it with him. As Kora looks over at him driving, she can see the desperate look in his eyes, the bead of sweat running down his cheek, and it's pissing her off. Her face has already changed, and she knows it. Kora is praying he doesn't speak. *Sam Jackson* is waiting in the wings like a hungry tiger stalking a wounded elk. She takes her phone out and begins playing on it, hoping maybe that will keep Mills from saying anything to her.

"We gotta find this girl," he said.

Kora doesn't respond, she just keeps playing on her phone. The rain continues to fall across the city, but that doesn't keep Mills from speeding. He's focused on the task at hand.

"Where should we look next?" he asked with desperation in his voice.

"I'm not sure," Kora responded without looking up.

"You don't seem to be taking this seriously rook. What's your problem?" he asked.

"Listen, it's better for both of us if we just finish this shift and go our separate ways," Kora warned.

"What's that supposed to mean? If you got something on your mind, let's hear it."

"Mills, I just want to finish my shift and go home. That's all I want," Kora advised.

"Well, you don't seem to be taking this seriously. A woman was taken. It's a damn shame," he said frustrated.

"Mills, do you know who Tamica Wrapp is?" she asked.

"No, should I?"

"Yeah, you should. She's the woman who was abducted just a few days ago. You and I spoke to the guy she was with when she was taken. She worked at the mall, remember?"

"Okay, yeah I remember that. Why are you asking?" Mills questioned.

"You and I have been called to at least fifteen different abductions. What makes this one different? Why are you going so hard on this one?" she asked.

"I don't understand. I'm following orders," Mills responds in a frustrated tone.

"No, you're not. You've seen several kidnappings and abductions. In the few months I've been paired with you, we've seen a lot of them. You show up, take some notes, and then dump them in a folder and file it into the cabinet that no one ever opens," she said angrily.

"Okay, well this one is getting worked right? So, what's the problem?" Mills asked.

"You're not dumb, okay. All these black women that have disappeared so far this year, and you're the one downplaying that shit each time. Your sorry ass don't move fast for nothing but a goddamn sandwich. Today, all of a sudden, you want to be thorough and on point. You want to give a damn today. This is why this country is what it is today. We're in a predominately black town and no one gives a damn when one of our sistas is taken, but you and your good ol' boys are ready to send the goddamn army into East Orange to look for this white woman,"

"Are you calling me a racist?" Mills angrily asked.

"You're either a racist, or an ignorant asshole. I'll let you decide which one," Kora blasts.

"This is why people are talking about you Merrit. You don't know when to shut up. I've tried to teach you how to be successful at this job, but you're a know it all. You don't want to listen to anybody. That's why your generation is stupid. You all think you have all the answers. But this time you've gone too far. I'm your senior training officer, and you're on probation. When we get back, I'm writing your ass up. If you're lucky, you'll just be suspended. "

"Is that supposed to scare me Mills? It doesn't. You don't give a shit about any of these black women that are disappearing in '*your*' town. Today, I saw you do something that I've never seen you do, you worked hard. You worked hard to find this white chick. It's important to you. The only difference between this case and the others we've had is that this chick is white," Kora raged.

"No, the difference is that the captain put us on the case. He wants this woman found a.s.a.p. I do what I'm told. Why can't you see that? Everything doesn't always have to be race – related. You have some real issues," Mills added

"Miss me with your bullshit Mills. You work in a city full of people you don't like. That's why you turn a blind eye to what's going on with the women here, and in every other city. You're an idiot, but you're not stupid. You're part of the problem,"

"You got a lotta balls talkin' to me like that Merrit. I'm done trying to show you the ropes. You clearly know everything!"

"I don't. But I've learned that people like you aren't gonna be able to show me much,!" She replies, cutting her eyes in his direction.

Kora went back to playing on her phone and Mills had no idea know what to say. He was angry and frustrated but doesn't really want Kora to know that she'd gotten under his skin that badly. As he drove back to the precinct, his body was jittery with anger. He can't even look over to her. It would be best to be quiet, but the superiority complex he has would never allow that.

"I'm not the one that put out an all-points bulletin for this woman. Maybe the powers that be felt she was a priority over your people," he said.

"There it is. I knew you had at least one typical dumb ass white privilege comment in you. You never let me down Mills. After you report me, maybe we should concentrate on work instead of talking to each other moving forward," she suggested.

"There probably won't be a *'moving forward'* for you, rook. After I report your black ass, you're either gonna be out of here, or a traffic cop," Mills tells her.

"I think there will be a *'moving forward'* for me actually," Kora responded.

"And how do you figure that?" he asked sounding puzzled but curious.

Kora calmly pressed a button on her phone and replays a recording of Mills saying *'after I report your black-ass, you're either gonna be out of here, or a traffic cop.'* She smiled and looked over at him. Mills took a deep breath. This was trouble he didn't need this close to retirement.

"Okay, okay, let's all calm down here. Just delete that and let's start over," he said.

"I don't think so. I'm calling the shots from here on. You're gonna do what I say. You understand?"

"Merrit, you're being unreasonable," Mills sputters.

"We can always just see how unreasonable the captain is after he hears what you said," Kora offered.

"What do you want," he asked with a hint of defeat in his voice.

"We just switched roles Mills. I'm your senior training officer now,"

Precinct 73 in New York City

No matter how much technology the country discovers, precinct 73 remained an outdated hole in the wall. Some police officers shared desks in a large open space. The old Coke machine looked like it'd been there for fifty years. The holding cell was full of men who had been arrested, some sitting on the old benches and some holding onto the bars. The man in charge was Pete Stapleton. He had over twenty-five years on the force. The undersized soft-spoken captain usually stays in his office, allowing the old precinct to almost run itself.

The door to the precinct opened, and in walked NBA Hall of Famer and New York Knick legend Jay Jones. He tried to come in low-key, but when the officers saw him, they all went crazy. They raced up to him, asking for pictures and autographs. The ever-gracious legend calmly smiled and took pictures with everyone. It's a routine he's gotten used to whenever he walks into a room. Jay retired twenty years ago, but his popularity has never dwindled. His sneakers still sell out constantly. He even had a reality show when he first retired that everyone still talks about. Jay bought so many franchises and startups that he put thousands of New Yorkers to work over the years. He's a giving icon, and everyone loves him to death. After a ton of handshakes, pictures, smiles, and autographs, the officers lead him up to the captains' office. When he walked in, Pete was genuinely happy to see him.

"Jay, it's been a long time," Pete said, shaking his hand.

"It's good to see you, Pete. It has been a long time," Jay agreed, sitting down.

"Well, as you can see, the place hasn't changed much," Pete said with a grin.

"You're the boss now. That's a big deal. How long you been running this place?"

"Rayton retired ten years ago. They basically had to force him to retire. The guy worked for fifty-seven years, retired, and had a stroke a week later," Pete continued.

"That old battle axe. As soon as he slowed down, huh?"

"Yeah Jay. I took over. It's been pretty easy,"

"Well, it's a good look for you. I remember when you were Rogers' partner. We didn't really see eye to eye all the time, but I respected you," Jay confessed.

"I appreciate that. Raj always talked about how you were a hero. It took me a long time to understand what he meant. But when he got jammed up and you helped him, I understood. I never forgot it. When we lost him, I was devastated. But I looked at you like family after that," Pete admitted.

"That's cool man. So, tell me how bad it is," Jay said, suddenly serious.

"Well, an officer stopped J.J. on the West Side Highway. He was doing just under a hundred miles an hour. When he pulled him over, He was high. The officer checked the car, and found a half an ounce of cocaine under his seat,"

"Damn. That boy is gonna be the death of me," Jay murmured and looked away.

"Yeah, that's pretty bad. But I contained the situation. Only the arresting officer knows who he was and doesn't want him to go down for it. I'm gonna make a call and get him into this private rehab facility, and as long as he stays for a week, this will go away," Pete promised.

"Thank God. I really owe you Pete,"

"Naw, it's no problem, Jay. You can take him home. Monday, he needs to report to the facility. I'll call you with the all the information,

They shook hands as Pete walked Jay down to the holding cells. Jay tried to hide his annoyance as he saw J.J. sitting in the corner. They released him into Jay's custody and within minutes, they were driving away.

"Let me guess, you don't want to talk about it right?" asked Jay.

"Not really," J.J. said.

"Why are you taking drugs?" Jay asked.

"I don't know. I don't know Dad.,"

"You've been distant for a while. Something's been off with you. I just couldn't put my finger on it. I never would've thought you were on drugs though. Are you depressed?" asked Jay.

"Sometimes,"

"Why son? You have everything. You got parents that love you, money, talent, what are you depressed about?" asked Jay.

"I don't know Dad. I can't really explain it," J.J. said.

"Try to,"

"I don't know. You're a boy scout. If you look up 'good guy' in the dictionary, there's a picture of you. My Dad is the ultimate good guy, and a hero to everybody. I can't live up to that. I'm not that person. I'm a disappointment,"

"You're not a disappointment. You don't have to live up to anything that I've done. You just have to be you. You're more talented than I'll ever be. You were reading music and playing piano at four years old. I shot a basketball. What you do is much more impressive. Stop worrying about what everyone thinks and concentrate on you. When I joined the league, the media went on and on about how ridiculous it was to have a 30-year-old rookie. I didn't listen to that trash. I raised you better than that," Jay said.

"I'm sorry Dad. I never want to embarrass you," J.J. said.

"I ain't embarrassed. I didn't get caught with coke, you did,"

J.J. laughed lightly as they pull up in front of his place.

"Dad, what about my car?" asked J.J.

"I'll get it tomorrow. But you're going to rehab Monday,"

"I don't want to go to rehab, Dad.,"

"You have to get better. You want to be just another singer/songwriter that overdoses?" Jay asked looking his son in the eye.

"No."

"Then you're going to rehab."

Mills sat at his desk annoyed, while filling out paperwork. The veteran can't get over the way his rookie talked to him. He felt disrespected, and to make matters worse, she had that recording of him. After sitting and stewing for about an hour, he looked around and called a number on his phone. After whispering, he finished and looked around before going back to his paperwork. As he wrote, Kora walked by, dropping her paperwork off to him. He looked up confused, and she just gave him a look and kept walking. Mills stared at her angrily until she was out of sight.

Kora smiled to herself as she got in her car. Things were so much easier now that she had power over Mills. She headed to the chicken spot to grab dinner before going home. Just as she turned onto the block the restaurant was on, her phone began to ring. A smile shot across her face when she saw the name.

"Hey, Uncle Jay," she said enthusiastically.

"Hey, Sweetie. What's goin on? Whatchu up to?" he asked.

"Just getting some wings on my way home. Gotta get that golden fried before The Knicks play tonight," Kora said.

"That's my girl."

"What about you? What's goin on with you Uncle?"

"Well, I got some bad news.

"What happened?" Kora asked.

"It's your brother. He got pulled over and the cops found coke in his car," Jay told her.

"Damnit. You gotta be kidding.

"I wish I was. Your brother needs help. I got him out of it, but he has to go to rehab."

"I know you got him out of it. I wish there was something I could do."

"There is Kora. You can make sure he goes to rehab and stays there."

"I'll definitely talk to him," she promised.

"Good. You okay? You sound like something is on your mind," Jay questioned.

"You know me so well, Uncle Jay,"

"Of course I do. What's going on?"

"I never got to meet my dad. He's gone and I know he's gone. My mom though: I don't know who she is, or where she is. I could be walking past her every day and not know it. I don't want it to bother me, but it does," she admitted.

"I wish I could help you. I really do. I've told you for years to go see his widow."

"She's not his widow Uncle Jay. They were married and she was cheating on him with his partner. They were separated. She's definitely not my mother," Kora responded.

"I know. They hadn't been together for years. Your Dad had to leave the country for a few years after he found out she was cheating. When he came back, I remember him seeing someone, but he missed Miesha. She did what she did, but she loved your dad. I still think you should go see her," Jay continued.

"For what? She's not my mom!"

"She was with your dad for a long time. You never know what you might get out of it. You want answers. You also want to know as much about your dad as you can find out. Why wouldn't you go see the woman that knew him best? Jay asked.

"Okay, okay, you have a point," Kora admitted.

"Of course, I do."

"You're too much. I'm walking into the chicken spot. I'll call you tomorrow. Love you Uncle Jay," she said.

"Love you Sweetie," Jay replied.

On the docks of Port Newark, Redd and some other longshore men were working. A large shipment of new cars had just come in, and they're driving them off of a large ship. The expensive luxury vehicles had traveled a long way. The first Thursday night of the month was 'shipment night.' At least five ships full of vehicles came in. They unloaded them and drove the vehicles onto trucks to be transported to different dealerships. There were five of them working, and it took hours. One of the guys, Dean, is working slowly: mainly because he's incredibly nosey. As the guys slowly drove the cars off the ships and onto the trucks, Dean noticed that Redd took the last car off every ship, stopped before he gets to the truck, takes a duffel bag from the trunk, and quickly puts it in his car. Dean watches him perform this routine with each ship. He's scared of Redd, but he's nosey as hell, so he wants to know what's going on.

Once they loaded all the cars, the guys took a much-needed break. Redd went to his car to make a phone call, while some of the guys sat and ate. Dean carefully watched every move Redd made. After about ten minutes, a black suv pulled up next to Redd's car. Two men got out and shook hands with him. Dean took out his cell phone and started taking pictures. Redd led them to his trunk and they examined the bags. They shared a few laughs before one of them gave Redd a big wad of cash. They talked for a few more minutes before the men drove off. A smiling Redd counted his cash before putting it away. Dean never took his eyes off Redd, watching his every move. When their break was over, he considered telling Redd what he saw. His first thought was to try and blackmail him, but his fear that Redd would beat him up kept him from doing that. He spent the rest of his shift thinking about what he saw Redd do.

At quitting time, Redd got in his truck and blasted his music. He lit up some weed and headed toward 1 & 9 South. He called Kora, but she didn't answer. They'd known each other since they ended up in the same group home as kids. They developed a friendship and he quickly put a stop to all of the bullying she was enduring. Redd was the first person to teach Kora how to fight. They were best friends for years, and finally kissed the night of their senior prom. They tried to date, but Kora went to college. Redd just stayed in the streets. Even though they dated on and off, once she became a cop Kora knew she couldn't see him anymore. Despite all her pleading, Redd was never going to leave the street life. Even though he made good money as a longshore- man, he made more just with the drugs he helped smuggle in through the port. He loved Kora and wanted to be with her, but he loved his money more. His new girlfriend Kenyatta knew what he did and didn't care, as long as he kept buying her stuff. Her nails and hair were always done, expensive clothes always on. She hated Kora because she knew how long they'd known each other, and she was jealous. As much as she gave him a hard time when it came to Kora, Kenyatta knew she couldn't beat her, so she just hassled him about her. Because Redd is a big intimidating man, most people don't mess with him. He'd been in and out of jail, but never for a long stretch of time. Every town has a guy like Redd: the one that everyone knows everywhere he goes. You know that guy that has more than enough money to move out of the hood, but instead just 'lives it up' on the block. He did his usual after work ritual, pulling up to the Muslim soul food spot on 4th avenue. After ordering his fried shrimp and fish platter, Redd always paid with a hundred-dollar bill and told the young woman to keep the change. As he walked out of the restaurant that sat in the Muslim neighborhood, he ran into a guy he knew from high school, Rashan. He asked Redd if he still helps smuggle things in from out of the country. It's one of those things that some people in some circles just know, but the no snitch rule kept him covered. Redd let him know that vehicles came in on the first Thursday of every month. After a quick conversation, he told Rashan to have his people load the contraband in the last vehicle on the fifth ship. It's a relatively light shipment, two kilograms of heroin. He told Redd that it's worth about seventy grand, and he'd give him ten grand for getting it off the dock. This was an old routine for Redd. He told Rashan to just make sure the stuff was in the car, and he shook his hand and rushed off. He had hot shrimp and whiting and this wasn't the time to hang around talking. Redd finally pulled up to his home on Arlington Avenue that sits across from an old ratty YMCA. As he walked up his stairs, he looked next door and saw Sascha, his 10-year-old neighbor, sitting on her porch with tears in her eyes. He can hear her mother and a man violently arguing inside.

"Hi Redd!" she says excitedly while wiping away a tear.

"Hey little mama, what's goin on?" he asked.

"Nothing much. Mom and her boyfriend are arguing again,"

"Dag, I'm sorry. I thought you'd be out here. I got you your favorite. You want to come in and play the X-Box?" he asked.

"You got me a bean pie?" she asked excitedly.
"I sure did. Come on," he said, opening his door.

"You're the best Redd: but you're coming up off of some of those shrimps you got," she said.

"Oh really? We'll see about that!" laughs Redd.

CHAPTER FOUR

Can't Hold Her Back

As Kora sits in her apartment eating her chicken wings, she thinks about calling J.J. She knows she should, even though she doesn't want to. He's just going to give her a bunch of excuses, and she's not in the mood to hear it. Besides, the game she's watching is good, and her chicken is amazing. She decided to call him tomorrow. As she puts her feet up on her couch, her phone begins to ring. It's a number she doesn't recognize. While rolling her eyes, she answers it.

"This is Merrit," she said.

"Yo, what's good Officer Merrit?" the voice asked.

"This Bit, from Rowley Park, remember?"

"Of course. Whatchu got for me Bit?" she asked.

"I know where that snowflake is," he laughed.

"Yeah? Okay, tell me where she is," Kora said.

"Hold up officer. We need something in return for this info yo,"

"And what would that be?" she asked.

"If we ever get jammed up, just help us out,"

"Done. Now tell me where she is?" Kora said.

"Aight officer. The casket boys took her. She's at an abandoned movie theater on Main Street: used to be the Ormont I think. They supposed to move her tonight by midnight. You won't ever find her after that," Bit responded.

"I owe you and your crew for this. I won't forget it," she said hanging up.

Within five minutes she's changed and rushing out the door. As her car zoomed out of the parking lot, she gets her captain on the phone.

"Who is this?" he said.

"Merrit sir. I need bac…"

"Let me tell you something Merrit, you don't get to tell anyone anything. You're a rookie. I don't care what you need. If you have a problem, tell your senior partner or wait til morning," he said before hanging up.

Kora was enraged as she sped toward Main Street. She considered calling it in to headquarters, but why should she? They'd only give her a hard time, and they probably would ignore her anyway. Still, she can't take on a whole gang by herself.

In a nice home on the quiet side of town, Mayor Brown was playing with his kids. He's chasing them all around the big, beautiful home that sat on the corner of East Orange and Bloomfield. His two boys were laughing and screaming as they ran all over the house from their dad who was making monster sounds. When he finally cornered them in the living room, his wife came in.

"You have a phone call Mr. Mayor," she says handing him the phone.

"Why didn't you tell them I was busy?" he asked.

"You need to take this call," his wife said.

He reluctantly takes the phone from her as she grabs the boys and takes them upstairs.

"This is Mayor Brown," he said, clearly annoyed.

"Hello Sir. I hope I'm not disturbing you,"

"Goddamn you Merrit! I told you not to keep calling me! Do I hafta change my number?" he asked.

"That's very mean sir. I have a situation I need some help with," she admitted.

"Listen, I'm not helping you! I don't care what it is. Now, I hafta go, okay?"

"That's fine. Have a good night then," Kora says, hanging up.

She parks behind the old Ormont Theater and makes her way onto the roof of the building. As she walks up to the old rickety door, her phone begins to buzz.

"Hello?" she answered.

"Even though I don't care, what did you need help with?" the mayor asked.

"Oh, well I was able to get the location of Vanessa Kirby. I called my captain to get some backup to the scene, but he couldn't get his thumb out of his ass, so he told me to go away. I figured it would look good for you if the mayor was on the scene when it went down, but since you're being mean I'm just gonna handle it," she said confidently.

"You found her?!" My God! Okay, tell me where! I'll have Swat and plenty of backup there. I can be out the door in two minutes," he said.

"No, you were being mean," she whispered.

"Merrit, I don't have time for your shit,"

"You're still doing it," she stated.

"Okay, okay. I apologize for being mean, okay?" The mayor pleads through a tight strain on his face.

"That's so much better. She's at the old Ormont Theater on Main Street. I'm going in now. I'll see you when you and my backup get here," Kora said.

"Why don't you wait?" he inquired.

"So, the good ol' boys can act like they found her? Nah. I'll see you soon,"

The mayor jumped up and grabbed his coat. He contacted the police captain and told him what was going on. Within ten minutes, the mayor, police, and swat were converging on the

Ormont. The police captain quickly warned the officers over the radio:

"Be alert, that idiot rookie Merrit went in there without backup. She's either dead or captured. Break off into groups of three and enter from each entry-point. Secure the victim, Vanessa Kirby, as quickly as possible. And regarding this gang that's inside, shoot to kill. Safeties off boys," he ordered.

As they pull up to the Ormont, everyone's eyes strain as they try to understand what they're seeing.

"Captain, look!" one of the officers says, pointing.

Everyone pulls up to see seven gang members on their knees on the sidewalk with their fingers interlocked behind their heads. Vanessa Kirby is sitting on the curb, and Kora has her gun drawn on the gang members. The local news followed the police there, and it's utter madness. As they all approach, Kora has the situation under control.

"There's three more gang members inside the building," she said.

"Why aren't they out here?" the captain asked.

"Because I had to shoot them," she replied.

The other officers get the gang members off the ground and into police cars quickly. An ambulance pulls up and the EMT's walk over to Vanessa Kirby and begin tending to her.

"This time you went too far Merrit. You had information on the whereabouts of Vanessa Kirby, and you didn't share it. You went to the location with no backup and no plan. You could've been killed, and you easily could've gotten the victim killed. You risked her life Merrit. You are finished!" the captain yells.

"I tried to tell you. You hung up on me,"

"Save it Merrit. I'll take your gun and badge now," he growled.

"Uh, excuse me captain," the mayor interrupted.

"Yes sir, Mr. Mayor," he responded, straightening up.

"I couldn't help but overhear your conversation. Is it true that Officer Merrit called you before she came here, and you told her that you didn't care what her issue was?" the mayor inquired.

"Oh, see I thought she…I didn't think…" the captain sputtered.

"No, you didn't think. This young officer is a hero, captain. And from now on if she reaches out to you for anything, I expect you to listen. Am I making myself clear?" the mayor asked, as he mean mugged the captain.

"Yes sir," the captain said looking down at his shoes and feeling embarrassed.

"Good. I would hate to have to make a decision regarding your position because of communication issues. Why don't you go check on Ms. Kirby," the mayor suggested.

"Yes sir," the captain responded, walking off.

"Well, Officer Merrit," the mayor said.

"Now you wanna be nice to me," Kora murmured.

"Oh, shut up. You're a hero. If you think you were getting looks at the precinct before, it's gonna be a lot worse now," he informed the rookie.

"I can deal with that," Kora responded with a mischievous look in her eyes.

"I know you can. So, you gonna tell me how you did it?" the mayor asked.

"Did what?"

"How'd you take down 10 armed men by yourself?"

"You really want to know?" she smiles.

"Yes," he says.

"I'll bet you do," Kora says while walking away from him.

The mayor's smile was huge. He was impressed and there was no hiding it. He watched Kora walk off until news cameras and media surround him. Kora smiled as she gives her statement on what happened and headed to her car. Vanessa Kirby stopped her to thank her before she headed out.

The next morning, the whole town woke up to the reports of what happened the night before. It's all over the news, and in the papers. Kora is being called a hero, but she doesn't like getting the recognition for finding a white woman when there are so many missing black women. She wakes up to see 10 missed calls and 30 text messages. Instead of responding to anyone, she throws on some clothes and heads to work early.

When she walks in, all of the officers applaud her. She forces a half smile and tries to make her way to the locker room. They continue to clap and cheer until she's out of sight. Frustration is setting in, as she doesn't want any type of recognition for what happened. She puts on her gym clothes as her phone continues to buzz and ring. Before she throws it into her locker, she looks and sees that it's Redd. She reluctantly takes his call.

"I don't wanna talk about it Redd," she says.

"Come on Special K, you a hero. I can't believe my girl is a hero," he says.

"First: I'm not a hero, second: I'm not your girl. Matter of fact, switch one and two around," she says.

"Don't be like that. Everybody's talking about this. You dismantled the casket-boys by yourself. Those little knuckleheads killed a lot of people. You gotta tell me what happened,"

"No Redd, I don't. I just did my job. There's nothing to tell,"

"Kora, it's me. Come on now, don't be like that," he says.

"Look, there was ten of them, only three looked like they ever shot a gun before. I came in hot and put those three down. The others gave up,"

"I'm proud of you Special K," Redd says.

"Well don't be. There are black women out here disappearing every day. Until we do something about that, there are no heroes,"

"I hear you. You gonna be okay?" he asks.

"I will be. The mayor made a promise to me. When he keeps his word, I'll be good," she says.

"So…I guess we're not celebrating?" Redd asks.

"You're such an ass. I'll call you later," Kora says.

She goes out to the gym and does her usual stretch routine. She's trying to clear her head. She puts her headphones on and begins to hit the punching bag. Finally, Kora begins to feel some peace. Her music takes her to another place. After a while, she doesn't even notice that she's punching the bag. This is clearly what she needed. Just as she really gets into it, there's a tap on her shoulder. She turns around and removes her headphones. It's the mayor, and he's there with another man.

"Good morning, Officer Merrit," the mayor says.

"Good morning, sir," she smiles.

"This is Kurt Vino. He's the chief of police," the mayor says.

"It's an honor sir," Kora says.

"No, the honor is mine Officer Merrit. The city is proud of the work you did yesterday. I wanted to come down and meet you personally. The mayor and I went through your file together today. You're the daughter of one of the greatest detectives that ever lived. Why doesn't anyone know this?" he asks.

"Well, I never met my father sir. It's not something I really talk about," she says.

"I understand. Well, I know you've only been an officer a short time, but what you've done can't be overlooked. You have a couple of options to think about. The mayor is starting up this abducted persons unit that you can be a part of, or I could find a spot for you on SWAT. Maybe you should think about it," says the chief.

"I want to help find more abducted persons sir," Kora says.

"I thought you might. Well, no one moves up as fast as you are about to. After reading about your dad, if you ever decide to take the detectives' exam, come see me and I'll waive the rule on years of service. You can take it whenever you're ready," the chief says.

"Thank you sir," she says.

"And what are you doing here today officer?" he asks.

"I start my shift in an hour," Kora says.

"No, you don't. You've earned a week off. Go do something, or do absolutely nothing," the chief says.

"Thank you sir," she says, shaking his hand.

The chief walks off leaving the mayor and Kora standing there.

"So, you still gonna change your number?" she asks.

"Shut up. You made me look real good, but you still get on my nerves," he says.

"Uh huh. You know, you've been really nice to me since we first met. Why?" Kora asks.

"You remind me of my daughter. We lost her years ago. She got on my nerves just like you do," the mayor admits.

"I'm sorry. But she must've been strong like me,"

"Yes, she was. Well, enjoy vacation Merrit. I'm sure we'll talk when you get back," he says.

"You know, you can call me Kora,"

"I'll do that," he says.

"What should I call you now?" she asks.

"Mr. Mayor," he says walking away.

The only person she actually told the whole story to was her Uncle Jay. She tells him everything. He loves hearing Koras' stories, and she genuinely loves telling them to him. As soon as she got to the car, she called him and explained the entire thing: from getting the call from Bit to the conversation with the mayor and the chief of police.

"Kora, I'm so proud of you," Jay says.

"Thanks Uncle Jay. That means a lot,"

"So, since you have a week off, come stay with me and Shel for the week. You love coming to the city. We can check on J.J. in rehab, walk around the city, and I got a couple of things I want you to do," he says.

"You know what? That sounds like fun. I'll pack a bag. See you in a couple of hours," Kora says.

"Great. Your room is exactly the way you left it,"

"I'm sure it is. I'll see you soon," she says.

Redd got ready to leave for work. After scarfing down some breakfast, he watched the news for a few minutes. The story about Kora kept coming on. Seeing her on television brought a smile to his face. He grabbed his keys and when he opened his door, Sascha's mother was standing there. She told him how much she appreciated him and how he always took Sascha with him, so she didn't have to hear them arguing. He told her it's no problem as he got in his car. Redd pulled off as Sascha watched his car speed toward William Street. She didn't notice that her boyfriend was watching from the window. As Redd headed toward 280 East, he called one of his coworkers to tell him he's going to be late. They were used to his routine, so it's no big deal. During the ride down to the docks he just couldn't get Kora off his mind. He remembered after he taught her how to fight, she went on to learn karate, and then trained in ultimate fighting. She tried to include him each time, but Redd wasn't giving up his street time to train with her. He knew it was real the last couple of times they sparred, and he had a whole lot of trouble with her. Of course, she didn't answer when he tried calling.

J.J. angrily walks into the Jacoby Rehabilitation Center with his father by his side. He had a long week ahead of him. Jay helped him fill out all of the paperwork. The intake process was quite a lot, but even though J.J. was impatient, Jay wasn't.

He told his son several times that everything was going to work out. Jay had developed a thick skin over the years but seeing his son in this condition had been very difficult for him. J.J. wanted to leave so bad, but he knew he'd end up in jail if he didn't go through with it. As they signed the last of the papers, a tear fell down J.J.s cheek. His father wiped his face and kissed his forehead, assuring him that after this, he would be fine. After two hours, they're finally ready to admit him. The nurses came out to get him and the director assured Jay that he was in good hands. As they walked him through the doors, he took one final look at his dad before he disappeared into the facility. Jay watched him and got a feeling in the pit of his stomach like he failed as a father. He knew after these six weeks; he needs to be a better father to his son.

The director led J.J. to his room and opened the door.

"J.J., the path to improvement starts now. For the next few days, you will crave drugs like never before, as the toxins make their way out of your system. It is important to be patient, think about the things you still want to accomplish in your young life, and concentrate on creating the steps to making that happen. This is Justin, he will be your roommate for most of your journey. This is his third time with us. Justin, make sure J.J. is comfortable and answer any questions he may have," the director said.

"Yes sir," Justin responded.

"There's a button over your bed you can press if you have an emergency. I will come check on you before dinner," says the director.

"Thank you," J.J. says while sitting on the bed.

He closes the door and J.J. doesn't move. He sits on the bed motionless and just stares off into space. His body is beginning to get cold. The reality of where he is begins to set in. He doesn't even realize that he's beginning to shiver.

"Hey, you okay man?" asks Justin.

He doesn't respond. J.J. just continues to stare off into space. He doesn't even notice that Justin is speaking to him. After going over all of the things he's done that's landed him here, his thoughts are all over the place.

"Hey, you're gonna be okay, you know," Justin says.

J.J. finally looks up at him and realizes he's not alone.

"Do you have any coke?" asks J.J.

"Man, you got it bad. Don't worry, this place can help you out a lot if you let it," says Justin.

J.J. isn't listening to anything Justin is saying. He's getting colder and colder. He takes a sweater out of his bag and puts it on, but it doesn't really help. He looks at the window and wonders if he can fit through it. His brain is racing. After a couple of hours, his mouth is extremely dry. Even though his thoughts are all over the place, J.J. tries his best to calm down. He takes some long deep breaths and attempts to relax.

"Hey man, its lunchtime. Come on, some food should help you a lot," says Justin.

He leads J.J. to the lunchroom and grabs him a tray. They get their food and sit at a table where an old white woman is sitting. She's talking to herself. J.J. tries not to stare but he can't help it.

"That's Jackie. We call her 'conspiracy woman.' She's always going on about something: the government, celebrities, some of everything. We ignore her mostly, but sometimes she'll say something interesting," says Justin.

"The government created the moon landing. They shot it in a studio. When Armstrong planted the flag, it was blowing all over the place. Well, there's no wind on the moon. How could that flag have been blowing? They never fooled me," says Jackie.

"See what I mean?" Justin asks.

J.J. doesn't respond. He just begins to eat his Salisbury steak and potatoes. Throughout dinner, Justin talks to him, but other than an occasional head nod, he doesn't respond to anything. Even though his mind is racing, he can't help but listen to the ravings of Jackie. As outrageous as they sound, everything she says makes you think. Throughout dinner, J.J. can't help but pay attention to every word she says. The old woman talks about a wide range of things, only speaking to herself. It's fascinating to him.

"The royal family wanted Princess Diana out of the way. People are really that naïve to think that a royal princess riding with a professional driver can just pass away in a single car accident. There were 14 cameras along the route that her car took, and two on the entrance of the tunnel itself. How was there no cctv footage at all? Diana was pregnant. The royal family didn't want the scandal on their hands. You think they were going to let royalty marry a non-Christian? The Duke of Edinburg got MI6 to do the dirty work. If it was a single car accident, why was there paint on the princess's Mercedes from a white Fiat? It was the same kind of car that was used by their security services to block roads for her Mercedes," says Jackie.

Justin just looks at J.J. and shrugs his shoulders. He hears this stuff all the time and he's used to it. He's cutting into his steak barely paying her any mind. J.J. on the other hand, is hanging off of her every word. If he could switch roommates for her, he would.

That night, J.J. goes into withdrawal. He's sweating profusely on his bed, shaking uncontrollably. Justin keeps an eye on him and makes sure his blanket stays on. He's pretty much seen it all, and he's all too familiar with J.J.'s situation. He gets a wet washcloth and places it onto J.J.'s forehead. After several minutes, he begins to shake a little less.

Kora uses her old key to get into her Uncle Jays house. She walks into the giant mansion and smiles. The large foyer is always well lit. Before she can even close the door, the maid is standing in front of her.

"Ms. Kora! It is so good to see you again. You have grown so much," she says.

"Madeline, how are you? It's been awhile," Kora responds.

"I am good Ms. Kora. I will take your bag up to your room. Your aunt and uncle are down in the game room," she says.

"Thank you so much," she says, heading down the long staircase to the basement.

When she gets downstairs, even though she used to live there, she still marvels at the wondrous basement. There's video games, a pool table, a ping-pong table, a single lane bowling alley, an 85-inch television, full bar, even a small theater. It puts a smile on her face every time. Seeing all of the great things there takes her back to the first time she came home with them. A 16-year-old kid that had been bounced around from foster home to foster home, seeing that basement the first time completely blew her mind. Her and J.J. used to spend hours in that basement. The giant pool out back was always fun, but the basement was their spot. Jay is sitting on the couch watching the Knick game, with a bowl of chips. Shel is sitting on the end of the couch reading a magazine. They light up when they see Kora, both getting up to hug her. She plops down on the couch in between them and digs right into Jay's bowl of chips.

"Senor Jay, should I make some appetizers for you guys?" asks Madeline from the staircase.

"You hungry sweetie?" Jay asks.

Kora is nodding her head wildly before he can even get the whole question out.

"Why'd I even ask? I know how greedy you are," Jay says.

"Yeah Madeline, hook something up please," he continues.

"Right away Senor Jay," she says.

"It's so good to see you Kora. You don't visit enough. And you have no excuse! You have a key," says Shel.

"You're right Auntie. It's been a little crazy though," Kora says.

"I'm sure it has. I mean, you are a hero now. What's that's like?" Shel asks.

"I'm no hero. I was just doing my job. It really wasn't as big a deal as they're making it out to be," Kora says.

"It is a big deal. You were on the news, in the papers. Don't downplay it. It's a great accomplishment," Jay says.

"Yeah, take it from someone that made sure everyone knew about his accomplishments," Shel says, pointing at the giant framed Jersey of his that hangs over the entranceway of the basement.

"Whatever Shel! Don't listen to her. She's the one that kept nagging me about pushing you too hard when I was teaching you karate. I'll bet it comes in handy on the job, doesn't it?" asks Jay.

"It sure does. All the time actually," Kora admits.

They spend a few hours laughing and watching the game. They tell old stories and eat a ton of food. By 1am, Shel says she's going to bed. Jay and Kora decide to hang out a little longer. They really miss each other.

"Okay, so what are you up to? I know you, Uncle," Kora says.

"Me? Why, nothing at all. Why I gotta be up to something?" he asks.

"Okay, talk to me," she says.

"Well, while you're here, I want you to pay your dads ex-wife a visit. Ex-wife, estranged, widow, whatever. I really want you to go see her. You're always asking me questions about your dad, why not ask the woman he was married to?" He asks, with an eyebrow raised.

"Oh God. You're not gonna let this go, are you?"

"No. And his old partner Pete Stapleton is now in charge of the 73rd precinct where your Dad worked. You should go talk to him as well. He called me today after he saw you in the news. It blew his mind when I told him who you were. Go to the 73rd and talk to him," Jay says.

"Any other things you need me to do while I'm in the city?" she asks.

"Not really. Make your way to the Bronx and get me a carrot cake from Lloyds before you head back," he says.

"You are unbelievable. When are we going to see J.J.?" she asks.

"We'll head over there Wednesday and see how he's doing," Jay promises.

On day two of J.J.'s rehab, he's craving drugs in a major way. His mouth is so dry; it hurts when he opens it. His head is hurting, and his stomach keeps contorting. He stays in bed for hours, skipping breakfast because it's just too much for him to get up. Even though he doesn't feel too much better by lunchtime, he forces himself to get up. He just has to hear what conspiracy woman will be talking about. One of the things that got him through the night was thinking about the off the wall things she said. Every wild conspiracy made sense. He can't wait to get discharged so he can have his cell phone back and look these things up. Justin helps him put his shoes on and button his shirt. Even though he feels sick, he's so excited to get back to the lunchroom. He makes his way down the hallway, barely even aware that Justin has his arm and is helping him walk. They get their lunch and sit at the table with Jackie. She doesn't acknowledge them; she just picks at her food while talking loudly.

"I've been homeless for 20 years. I've seen a lot of things. That's why they always come around and shut me up. I know too much. There's the black girl that does that rap music: her name is Nicki Minaj. I like black people, I swear I do, but you know they can be slow sometimes. They're so slow that they don't even realize that Minaj's whole persona is an alter ego for that Jay-Z guy. She provides the eye candy, and he provides the rapping. All her songs are his voice, sped up to sound like a woman. If you don't believe me, slow down her songs, they'll sound just like him. And if you speed up his songs, they'll sound just like her. Those people are so gullible," she says loudly.

J.J. has a wide smile on his face. He's been looking forward to this since yesterday. He sits there eating and hanging off of her every word. He makes a mental note to speed up a Jay Z record and test this theory as soon as he gets out.

"Hey man, you look like you're feeling a little better," says Justin.

"I do feel a little better today," J.J. admitted reluctantly.

"Good. It takes a minute, but you won't even crave drugs soon. I'm glad you're getting better," Justin encouraged.

"Thank you, buddy.

"*Pokemon Go* is a spy program created by the government. Right in the so-called game's terms of service it says you've allowed it to give any information about you to government or law enforcement officials. The game was designed by a company called Niantic. They have ties to the government intelligence apparatus. By harvesting the images of all the people playing the game, the CIA has surveillance all over the world. This is how stupid people are! It says it right in the terms of service!" Jackie said.

"Wow. I need to delete that app off my phone," says J.J.

"You can't really believe the stuff she says," Justin warned.

"Why not?"

"She's crazy man. For God's sake, we call her conspiracy woman. Years of drugs have fried her brain. Trust me, those are the rants of a lunatic, said Justin.

"Maybe," J.J. responded.

CHAPTER FIVE

Turning Redd

Kora took a deep breath after parking her car outside of Precinct 73. She always said she would never set foot in the precinct that caused her father so much heartbreak. She got out of the car and reluctantly walked up the stairs. Kora may be a tough, no-nonsense person, but she's all woman. Her curvaceous five-foot eleven frame can't be ignored. She walked into the precinct with her head held high. All the officers turned and stared as she stopped at the information booth.

"I shouldn't have worn a dress today," she said, while looking at all the eyes on her.

She waited up front for about five uncomfortable minutes. A lot of thoughts were going through her mind. She looked at every older cop as if they did something to her father twenty years ago. She read everyone's name tag in a search for Marie, the partner he had that slept with his wife. Pete finally came down the stairs and saw Kora. His eyes almost bulged out of his head. He walked up and awkwardly hugged her.

"My God, you look just like him," Pete says.

"I do?" Kora asks while politely ending the embrace.

"Yes, you do. Follow me, my office is upstairs," he says.

Everyone watched them until they went into his office and out of sight. In Pete's office, there are so many pictures of her dad. Kora looked around in amazement at the pictures of Pete and her dad in uniform. It took everything in her to hold back the tears she felt.

"Your dad was my first partner. He taught me everything. He was an amazing man. There was nothing he couldn't do," says Pete.

Kora was so busy taking in all the pictures that she didn't even hear Pete. He looked up and saw her admiring the pictures of her dad: with Pete, shaking hands with the mayor, getting the key to the city, the smile on her face was from ear to ear. Pete smiled and waited patiently for her to take it all in.

"When Jay called and told me about you, I couldn't believe it. I wish I would've known you existed. None of us would've left you in those foster homes if we knew about you," says Pete.

"It's okay. I appreciate that though. But please Captain Stapleton…"

"Call me Pete," he said.

"Okay Pete, tell me about my dad. I know all the basics, but tell me some real things," Kora requested.

Pete leaned back in his chair, looked up in the air and smiled.

"He was a great poker player. He routinely beat all the other guys out of their money. He was selfless. There was a homeless guy that lived on the corner of this station. Your dad, well, Raj, used to pay him a hundred dollars a week to get his lunch for him and bring it here to him every day. He loved Mountain Dew: drank one every day. He was always the smartest guy in the room. Half of the cases he solved were just him walking into a crime scene and breaking down what happened. He hated authority. Our captain hated him, and he hated the captain. The older guys here didn't like how quickly he moved up the ranks, but he was the best detective anyone had ever seen. He was big and strong, but soft-spoken. I was heart-broken when he died," he said.

"Do you know anything about who my mother is?" she asked

"I assumed Miesha, Roger's wife, was your mother," Pete said.

"No, she's not. They were apart when I was created."

"Oh, I have no idea. If anyone knew that, it would hafta be Jay. Those two guys were inseparable. And Raj wasn't the type of guy to see random people. Maybe your uncle can remember," he says.

"Thanks Pete," Kora grinned.

"Of course. And I have something for you.

Pete walked over to his cabinet and started rummaging around in it. He came back and handed Kora a small box. She opened it to see her fathers' badge, number 1112008. She stopped trying to hold back and just lets her tears go.

"Oh wow, I'm sorry. I wasn't trying to upset you," Pete shifts nervously. Seeing her cry was getting to him.

"You didn't. This is the happiest I've been in a long time," Kora answered as she tried to smile and pull herself together.

"Without him, I would never have lasted on the job as long as I did. I know you're on the job in Jersey. If you ever need anything, you've got family here," Pete told her and offered his fist for a bump.

"Thank you, Pete, for everything," Kora replied, awkwardly fist bumping him.

"Of course," Pete smiled, glad the awkward moment was behind them.

"Can I ask you something?" Kora inquired.

"Anything," he replied.

"His partner after you, Marie: The one that was having an affair with his wife. Whatever happened to her?"

"Marie was killed on the job five years after your father was killed. She was trying to stop a bank robbery and was shot," Pete responded and held her gaze.

It's Wednesday afternoon and J.J. feels pretty good. He and Justin are sitting in their room playing chess. The brightly lit room is beginning to almost feel like home to him. For the first time in months, he's not craving drugs. As lunchtime quickly approaches, there's no hiding J.J.'s excitement. *What will Conspiracy Woman say today?* He's like a little kid.

"Come on Justin, it's lunchtime," he says.

"Uh huh. You keep hanging off all that crazy stuff Jackie says, and people are gonna start thinking you're crazy," says Justin.

J.J. almost wants to run to the lunchroom. Listening to the ravings of Jackie has almost given him a sense of worth. In his mind, Jackie may be crazy, but she's definitely seen and experienced things that most people haven't. He and Justin get their trays of food and sit at the table where Jackie is sitting. J.J. enthusiastically says 'hi' to her, but she doesn't respond.

"One of Brittney Spears backup singers can sound just like her. She's actually better than her. Her name is Myah Marie. If you don't believe me, just listen to the songs *Passenger* and *Alien*. It's obviously not Brittney Spears singing. Myah Marie sang 7 out of 12 of her songs on her 2011 album. The studio paid her to sound like Spears," Jackie says.

"That's really interesting. I'm a singer, so anytime I learn something I don't know, it's fascinating to me," J.J. admits.

She doesn't even look in his direction. As J.J. waits impatiently for Jackie to spit out more random theories, she just sits and stares off into space. After about fifteen minutes, he realizes he's not going to get any more today. His only hope is that she says more at group therapy later that afternoon. Disappointed, he heads back with Justin to get a quick game of chess in before his group therapy session. He genuinely feels better and he's in good spirits. He's seen some of the extreme cases at the facility, and he genuinely doesn't want to ever be one of them.

After a spirited game of chess, J.J. sits at the table and writes in his journal: another non-negotiable activity assigned to him by the facility director. He's actually enjoyed writing his daily feelings in it. In the three days he's been there, he's written down the things he wants to accomplish, his biggest regrets, even things he's thought about, but never told anyone. He's making amazing progress because he really wants to. He's beginning to realize that he doesn't have much to be depressed about. There are people that would give anything to be in his position. For the first time in a while, J.J. is smiling.

Port Newark, New Jersey. The foreman for the pier is sitting in his office, looking down on Redd and the other long shore-men as they slowly drive the vehicles off the first ship, and load them one by one onto trucks. He sips his coffee with his feet up as he watches his guy's work. Thursdays are his favorite days. It's the day that Redd pays him 400 dollars to look the other way when he gets his side action coming into the port. As he snacks on a donut, he watches the guy's work.

Redd removes the bags from each car and loads them into his car. He knows when they unload the last ship; there should be bags in the last two vehicles because of Rashans' heroin. They unload luxury vehicle after luxury vehicle.

"I'll get the last two out," Redd announces.

"Yeah, yeah," a couple of the guys say.

He drives the next to last car off the ship and pulls it up near his car. He pops the trunk and hurries over to it. He reaches in, but the trunk is empty! He feels around frantically, but there's nothing to find. Confused, he pulls the car onto the truck, and goes back aboard the ship to get the last car. He drives it up to his vehicle and does the same thing. He gets the same result. The last car is completely empty. He gets on his phone quickly to try to see if there was an issue loading on the other side. Of course, no one is answering the phone. He's trying not to panic, but he knows this is a major problem.

His foreman watches from the window as the dark suv pulls up, and four men get out. He could see Redd hand them four bags. They had a clear look of confusion on their faces. One of them appeared to make a phone call, and Redd was clearly arguing with the men. Before his foreman could fully grasp what was happening, one of the men punched Redd in the back of the head, dropping him to his knees. The men then all kick and stomp on him. His foreman hopped up and rushed down the stairs. His coworkers all watched but none of them helped Redd. By the time his foreman got outside, the men had pulled off. He went over and helped Redd to his feet, but he was wobbly.

"What happened? Are you okay?" asked his foreman.

"Yeah. I gotta get outta here though," he responded.

Redd got in his car and tried to take some deep breaths, but that was hard for him to do without coughing. He knew he was in big trouble. He took some tissues out of his glove compartment and wiped the blood from his mouth as he drove away from the port. His phone began to ring. He looked down and saw it was Rashan. Redd knows he can't answer. As much as he doesn't want to, he called Kora.

"What Redd? I'm at my uncles house in New York," she answered.

"That's cool. I need a favor," he says.

"Of course you do,"

"I'm serious this time,"

"What's wrong Redd?" she asked.

"It's better if you don't know. I can't go home. I need somewhere to lay low for a day,"

"Okay, well, go to my place. Park in my spot," she said.

"The key is still in the same spot?" he asked

"Yeah. If you're in trouble, tell me what's going on?"

"Kora, it's better if you don't know. You're gonna hafta trust me. I'll call you tomorrow," he said.

"Fine. I'm coming home tomorrow then," she said.

"Kora, you don't hafta…"

"I'll see you tomorrow," she said, hanging up.

She puts the phone back in her pocket and smiles at Jay and J.J. They're in the visitors' room at the rehab facility. Her and Jay are genuinely happy at the progress J.J. has made. He's smiling, there are no bags under his eyes, and he's talking about his future. It's amazing to them how he's improved so quickly. As their hour is just about up, they both Hug J.J. as they all stand up. Jay tells him he'll be there to pick him up in three days. As he's led back to his room, the director walks out with Jay and Kora. He tells them that no patient he's ever had has experienced such a fast turnaround. He's impressed. When they get in the car, Kora lets Jay know that she's going to have to cut her vacation a little short.

"You said you were staying til Sunday," he says.

"I know. Something came up. I'm sorry. I'll come back next month though," she promises.

"Sure you will. You know what we're gonna hafta do then…"

"What are we gonna hafta do Uncle Jay?"

"We're gonna ride over to Miesha's house now then," he says.

"Oh, come on! She's not my mother, you know," Kora protested.

"She was married to your dad. We're going,"

Kora sits quietly, annoyed at her uncle for forcing her to do this. Yes, this woman was married to her father. She may have stories, or even pictures, but she's not her mom. This woman cheated on her father with his partner. That's what ultimately broke him and caused him to snap. Kora has nothing but resentment for this woman. She knows that with her quick temper, she's gonna blow up on this person. Why is Jay pushing this so hard?

The twenty-minute drive feels like three hours to her. She's uncomfortable and nervous, patting her leg throughout the ride. She can't think of what to say to get out of it.

"I met with Pete. Wasn't that enough?" she asks.

"No," laughs Jay.

"Listen, do you remember my dad dating anybody before he died?"

"I don't think so. He came back from Brazil for that last case. And he was only here for a few weeks before he was killed. I do remember we were out one night, and he ran into this woman he liked. We ended up having dinner with her and her friends. I don't remember her name though. I'm bad with names of people I just met, let alone 20 years ago," he says.

"Yeah, I understand that," she says.

They park in front of the brownstone in Park Slope. The garden is full of fresh strawberries. There's an expensive looking Porsche coupe sitting in the driveway. Kora tries to talk Jay into just pulling off, but he's not hearing it. They sit in front of the house for several minutes as Kora tries to collect her thoughts. For Jay, it's not a simple thing either. He hasn't spoken to Miesha in a few years. He didn't appreciate what she did with the whole cheating thing, but he had his own infidelity that he was dealing with, so he understood how it could happen. Jay didn't call ahead, and never told Miesha that Kora exists.

Although they had been separated for years, Miesha made out well from Rogers' death. He had a million-dollar insurance policy, and she was the only beneficiary. She never remarried: instead, she spent 10 years traveling the world and creating her own adventures. Instead of moving out of the home they shared, she just paid it off. Miesha now leads a modest life. She doesn't work. Her life consists of girl's nights with her friends and tea with her other friends. As Jay and Kora walk up to the door, they can hear women's voices inside.

"Maybe this isn't a good time Uncle Jay," says Kora.

He gives her a look before ringing the bell. The door opens and Miesha looks at Jay stunned.

"Jay? Oh my God! Get in here," she says.

As they walk into the house, she hugs him tightly. The other women in the house that are sitting on the couch instantly pop up. They're not sure if their eyes are playing tricks on them.

"It's good to see you Esh," Jay says.

"I can't believe it's you. It's like you to just pop up after all this time though," she says.

"Girls, this is Jay," she says.

"We know who he is!" They say running over to meet him.

"And this is…I'm sorry, I didn't get your name," Miesha says.

"I'm Kora," she says.

"Nice to meet you. And this is Kora, girls. Jay, Kora, this is Teri and Consuelo," she says.

"Nice to meet you both," they say.

"Jay, it's wonderful to see you. How's Shel? How's J.J.?" Miesha asks.

"Everybody's good. I was hoping we could talk," he says.

"Of course. Girls, lets pick this up tomorrow," Miesha says to her friends.

"I know you don't think we're leaving now that *the* Jay Jones is here," says Consuelo.

"Yeah, that's not happening," says Teri.

"Oh God. Well, go to my room then," Miesha says frustrated.

As Teri and Consuelo walk upstairs, Miesha leads Jay and Kora over to the living room couch. She sits in a big wicker chair facing them.

"Jay Jones, you finally came to see me after all this time. I'm glad you did," Miesha says.

"It looks like you're doing okay for yourself," he says.

"It was hard losing him Jay. I was hurt for a long time. He left me so much though," she says.

"You have a nice home," says Kora.

"Thank you. You said your name was Kora. How do you know Jay? You look familiar," says Miesha.

"Jay's my uncle," Kora says.

"Your uncle? Jay's brother was in jail until about 10 years ago. How is that possible?" Miesha asks.

"I'm not his brother's kid," says Kora.

"Oh, so he's not really your uncle, you just call him that," Miesha says nodding.

"Well, I guess. To me, he is though. I'm his best friend's daughter," Kora says.

"His best friend? He's only had one best friend throughout his life. His best friend was…" Miesha begins.

"My name is Kora Merrit," she says.

"Miesha looks at the young woman in her home confused. Her brain can't seem to process what's happening. Her first thought is: *'why is this woman saying I gave birth to her? She's not my kid.'* After a minute of processing, she realizes what's happening. She looks hard at Kora's face and sees her late husband. She takes her hand and places it on top of her head, closing her eyes. You can hear the gasps from Teri and Consuela who are hiding at the top of the stairs. She can tell that this woman is somewhere around 21 years old. It makes sense now.

"I…um…I see. And who is your mother?" she asks.

"I don't know. I've been trying to find out for twenty years," Kora says.

"So, are you after money?" Miesha asks.

"You're kidding right? I don't want your money. Uncle Jay made me come here. I didn't want to," she says.

"She doesn't want money Esh. I just thought you should meet, that's all. I thought you'd want to know that Roger had a daughter," Jay says.

"We were supposed to have kids. I always thought we would," says Miesha.

"Was that before or after you cheated on him with his partner," Kora asks.

"You don't get to come around after 20 years and judge me. Your father was the greatest detective this city ever had.

Do you know what that means? Let me tell you: every tough case this city ever got was his. Every high-profile case this city had was his. Whenever the mayor needed help, he called Roger. First, he was only home 2 days a week, then one. Next thing you know, he forgets a birthday, then an anniversary. Before you know it, a month has passed, and you only shared one meal together. Every movie that you want to see, every show you want to go to, you have to ask a girlfriend. I'm the one that helped put him back together after he was shot by a gang member and stabbed by a hit-woman. I was there when he tore his knee in college, ending his football career. I helped him through his depression, the drinking, and the AA meetings that no one knew he was going to. I was by his side riding and dying no matter how dark it got, so don't judge me," Miesha says.

"Whatever," Kora responds uninterested.

"I made a terrible mistake. I've regretted it my whole life. After Roger and I separated, I realized how much I had messed up. The last time we spoke, I told him to be careful. I told him to call me back so we could talk. I didn't wait either. I called him back. I was gonna tell him to come home. I was too late though. I...was...too late," says Miesha.

"Well, we don't want to keep you. I know you have company," Jay says.

"I do. Girls: Jay is ready to take a few pictures with you," Miesha yells out while staring at Kora.

"Teri and Consuelo came barreling down the stairs toward Jay with their phones out. He gets up and meets them halfway.

"Why don't you follow me," Miesha says, leading Kora to the basement.

She opens the door and Kora's eyes widen. There's her dad's old cop uniform in a frame, hanging on the wall. Under it are at least a hundred newspaper clippings of his various exploits. There's a photo album of him and Miesha. There's videotapes of him playing basketball, receiving commendations, even just lounging around. Kora doesn't even ask permission before she pops a tape in the VCR.

"You really are your fathers' child," she said.

"Yes I am," Kora said as she, hit play.

"It hurts me just as much seeing you as it does you seeing me. I made a mistake, but he was everything to me," Miesha admitted.

"I think I'm starting to understand. I never got to meet my father, so I'm extra protective of him," said Kora.

"I get it. I've prayed for forgiveness every day for twenty-five years because of my stupid decision. Roger didn't deserve what I did. I guess I was just so frustrated. But that's old news. Everything happens for a reason," says Miesha.

"And how do you figure that?"

"If I didn't make that stupid mistake, you never would've been born," Miesha pointed out.

Kora looked over at her, but didn't say anything. She'd never thought about that. She watched her father on the old videotape with a sense of pride. He was just talking to some friends after playing basketball: but seeing him relaxed, laughing, and just being himself, gave Kora a whole different side of him. She sat on the edge of the couch, watching alertly.

"Can I keep this tape?" Kora asked.

"No," Miesha says.

"Can I take any of these tapes with me?"

"No, you can't. I do have something you can take with you though," Miesha said, opening a closet door.

She pulled a big tote from the closet and put it in front of Kora.

"What's that?" asks Kora.

"I don't know. I never opened it. He always said it was for his child. And he said if anything ever happened to him; give it to his child when they turn 18. When he died, I just left it in the closet. It's been in there for twenty years," Miesha stated.

Kora picked up the big tote and followed Miesha up the stairs. Jay was sitting on the couch, laughing with Teri and Consuelo. He's telling old stories and was in his element. When he saw Miesha and Kora coming up from the basement, he got up and went over to them.

"What's in the tote?" he questioned.

"I have no idea. Your friend left it to his child," Miesha responded.

"Really? Wow. That sounds like him. I'll take it out to the car. Esh, it was good to see you. Ladies, nice to meet you both," he said, hugging Miesha and carrying the tote outside.

"Well, this was interesting," Miesha said.

"Yeah," agrees Kora.

"And what do you do exactly?"

"I'm a cop," she answered proudly.

"Of course you are," Miesha lightly smiled.

"Let me give you some advice young lady: all the hate and rage you have in your heart, lose it. It's just going to hold you back. The reason your father was so successful at his job was because he had razor sharp focus. He didn't get emotional. He was always calm and relaxed, and that's why he was the best damn detective this city ever saw. He worked that way for 20 years, and he never failed at his job. And you know what? The one time he went out there not focused, emotional, angry: he got himself killed. If your goal is to be half as good as Roger was, lose the attitude," Miesha advised.

"Thanks for the tote," Kora whispered on her way out the door.

Miesha pulled an old detective badge out of her pocket and placed it on top of the tote that Kora carried . They lightly nodded at each other as Kora continued down the stairs.

She gets in the car and Jay pulled off. He's laughing.

"Was that so bad?" he asked.

"I guess not," Kora admitted.

"What do you think is in the tote?" asked Jay.

"If it was anything of value, she would've kept it," she said.

Inside the Jacoby Rehabilitation Center, J.J. just finished his group therapy session. The counselor complimented him on the great progress he'd made. He eagerly headed down to the lunchroom with Justin. His white jumpsuit is at least two sizes too big, as the cuffs of his pants lightly touch the ground when he walks. He now greets other patients whenever he walks past them. He and Justin get their trays and take their usual seats at the table with Jackie. She's staring into space as usual. J.J. watches her intensely while he eats, waiting for the show to start. He only has a couple of days left to enjoy conspiracy woman.

"In 1962, Marilyn Monroe supposedly overdosed at her house. They said she committed suicide. They called it suicide by barbiturates. If that was true, why were there no traces of pills in her stomach? She had a lot of well-known plans for her future, so why would anybody believe she killed herself? The first guy on the scene was an LAPD Cop named Clemons. He said the body looked staged. The police were called hours after Marilyn Monroe was found dead. And how about this; wouldn't someone who took dozens of pills have a cup or some water nearby? She didn't. What happened was, she was messing with Robert Kennedy and his brothers. They knew she was going to tell everybody eventually, so they killed her. The Kennedys have had bad luck ever since," Jackie said.

J.J. smiled a big smile as he went back into his sliced turkey dinner. Sometimes she gives him two, sometimes one, but either way he's always satisfied. Before he could even process the new conspiracy he'd been given, Jackie spits out an unexpected one:

"Jay Jones was everybody's hero. He was New York's white knight. He was the country's role model. I was getting my hip replaced at Mercy General back twenty-five years ago when his wife was having her baby. Well, I saw them take the baby out of her room: and I can tell you, that baby was dead. But two days later, when I was leaving the hospital, he was leaving with his new son. The rich can get away with anything!" she said.

"What are you talking about?" J.J. asked loudly.

He jumped up out of his seat and rushed over to Jackie, yelling and grabbing her by the shirt. As she yelled out, the orderlies came running up to them, grabbing and restraining J.J. He fought and struggled but there's too many of them.

"Why would you say that?! Why?!" J.J. screamed as they carried him down the hall. He struggled to no avail. They finally dumped him in a small, padded room and locked the door. He banged on the door screaming for several minutes. Finally, he slumped down, stared at the padded wall and tried to process what he heard.

Kora got in her car as soon as they got back from Park Slope. Even though the getaway was cut short, it almost feels like she spent it with her father. Looking over at Roger's badge on her passenger seat is keeping Kora smiling. It's also making her wonder what could be in that tote. What could he have possibly left for a child that he never knew he was going to have? The curiosity is almost enough to make her pull over. With her thoughts all over the place, Kora finally pulls into her parking lot. She grabs the duffel bag and pulls the tote out, carrying them both to the door. The brightness of the full moon shines down like a spotlight. Struggling to put her key in the door, someone grabs Kora from behind and throws her to the ground. The tote crashes violently as Kora struggles to quickly free her arms from the duffel bags straps. Looking up, her eyes are greeted by three men in ski masks looking down at her. Once she gets her arms free, Kora quickly stands up.

"Okay, let's go then," she says angrily.

The men rush her wildly. The first one threw a punch and she quickly grabbed his arm, kicking him in the chest twice. In the middle of that, one of the men punched her hard in the face. She calmly backed up, blocked his next punch, and grabbed his arm, jumped in the air and rolled, twisting his arm as she does it. Kora took a kick to the back that almost put her on the ground. She turns around, knocking down his second kick attempt, and elbowing him in the face. The numbers game isn't in her favor, and they're starting to over-power her. As she fights with one guy, another one grabs her at the waist, holding her. She starts to take hard shots. She could feel herself getting a little woozy. Before she passed out, the door opened and Redd came running out. He attacked the men and that backed them up temporarily. Once they regroup, Kora shook the cobwebs out. Her and Redd quickly gained the upper hand on the assailants. They run to their dark van and try to quickly pull off. As they rushed out of the lot, Kora saw a bumper sticker on the van. It said, *'Ray's Fish House.'*

"That bastard," Kora mumbled just loud enough for Redd to hear.

"You know who it was?" asks Redd.

"I think so. I knew it. I told you, you stalk me!" she says, grinning while holding her ribs."

"Whatever. I'll bet you're happy I was stalking that ass," Redd laughs.

"Oh, shut up,"

They pick up her stuff and head inside.

Kora gets ice out of the freezer and wets some washcloths. They get on the couch, and she tends to Redd's wounds. After removing his shirt, his body looks like that of a man that's been roughed up twice in a short time. She puts a small bag of ice under his eye and then begins cleaning his cuts.

"Thanks Redd," she says.

"All good Special K," he replies.

The two begin to kiss passionately. As soon as Redd reached for her breasts, she grabbed his hand and stopped him.

"Nope. I'm going to bed," she says, getting up and walking towards her bedroom.

"Whatchu mean?! I can't come with you?" Redd asked.

"No Redd. My bedroom is for my man," she answered calmly.

"What the hell are you talking about? You don't have a man," he said.

"Exactly," Kora responds, closing her door.

Redd rolled his eyes and tried to get comfortable on the couch.

CHAPTER SIX

Aiding and Abetting

The next morning Kora woke up sore. She climbed out of bed and put her robe on, then headed out to the living room. Redd was still asleep on the couch. After turning on the coffee maker, the sound of Redd yawning echoed throughout the apartment. Kora looks at the tote; in all the excitement last night there was never a chance to open it. After picking it up and quietly carrying it to her bedroom, Kora stares at it for a couple of minutes. She takes the top off of the tote and looks at the numbered dvds, confused. It's at least 20 of them. She quickly puts the first one in her dvd player and closes her door. There's Roger sitting in a chair, looking directly into the camera. Kora's hand goes to her mouth as she watches emotionally.

"My beautiful daughter or my handsome son, I want you to know that I'm proud of you. You're an adult now, and I wish I was around to be there with you on the next part of your journey. If you're my child, you've probably found your way into law enforcement. It's what we do. I'm very good at my job. It took a long time, a lot of training, and a lot of focus. There are two types of people in this world: the ones who show up to work every day right on time, do their job adequately, and go home. Then there are the other kind: the one that always gets to work early, never misses a single detail, and is always the person in the room that everyone looks at for guidance. If you're carrying the last name *'Merrit,'* you've got a legacy to uphold. Unfortunately, if you're watching this, it means that I'm no longer here.

He picked up a Mountain Dew and took a big swig, wiped his mouth, and put it down. Kora smiled slyly as he continues.

"Don't worry, I would never let a thing like death keep me from making sure that you ultimately become a better detective than I ever was. I'm serious, you will be. I've been keeping this box for you years before you were even thought about. I've made you different dvd's that are gonna teach you everything you need to know about being the best detective you can be. Watch them all and study them. Go out there and change the world. It's gonna start by you changing yourself,"

Kora stared at the screen in shock. This man that she grew up idolizing but never met, was everything she'd always thought he was. He thought of everything. She looked at a couple of the dvd labels, *'how to break down a crime scene,' 'how to find a clue when there are no clues,'* and *'how to tell a guilty person.'* Kora is realizing that her life may have just changed. For a second, she contemplates if she needs these dvd's. She's planning to join this new abducted persons unit, she has a good relationship with the mayor, and she's moving up faster than anyone. She's already a name around the department. Is this what she really wants?

After five minutes, she knows she's going to go through these dvds and study them. She has three days of vacation left and she wants to dedicate them to breaking down the dvd's, but she knows she needs to help Redd first. She walks out of the room to see him lying on the couch texting.

"Okay, Redd, what's going on?" Kora asked.

"I won't go into detail, but every other Thursday I get some items at the port. Yesterday those items didn't show up. It looks like they were shipped to me like every week, but they never made it there or something. I'm the one taking the fall for it. And if I don't come up with them, or the 200 grand in product that's missing, somebody's gonna put holes in me," he says.

"Items, ugh, you make me sick. Anyway, how do you know these 'items' didn't make it to the port?"

"Kora, I take them out the trunks of the foreigns that come in. They weren't there,"

"So, the senders never shipped them then,"

"They say they did. And they do too much business to lie,"

"Okay, so maybe something else happened,"

"Like what?" Redd asks.

"I don't know. Maybe one of your long shore-man buddies got to it before you did," Kora suggested

"Naw, they know better. It's only five of us."

"Tell me about them," she says.

"Aint much to tell. It's me, then there's Joe: he's a family guy, works a lot of overtime. Barry is a quiet guy, works his time and gets out of there. George is a jokester. I think he has four kids from four baby mamas, but he takes care of them. Dean is a quiet guy; he's nosey as hell though. That's it,"

"Do they all know when you get your items?" Kora asked.

"Well yeah, but I mean, I don't think…"

"I know Redd. You never think,"

"Come on Special K. Don't be like that," he said

"Whatever. Where does Dean live?" she asked.

In New York City, Jay received a phone call from the rehab center. They let him know that J.J. took a step backwards and he was going to need to stay a few extra days. The director told him that J.J. tried to attack a woman in the lunchroom. Inside the center, in that same small, padded room, J.J. was still sitting in the same place. He couldn't understand why Jackie was saying that stuff. Maybe every conspiracy she'd mentioned was a complete lie. Maybe there was just a kernel of truth in everything she said. He had so many different thoughts.

'If Shel isn't really my mother, who is? Why would dad keep this from me? Naw, that woman is crazy. I never shoulda let her get to me like that. She's a crazy old lady. What the hell is wrong with me? She does these things for entertainment.

He looked around the room for a way out. There was nothing in the room to use. The ceiling was too high, and there wasn't anything loose anywhere. He started fiddling around with the door. Somehow, he managed to slide the deadbolt from his side of the door. J.J. quietly walked down the hallway peeking into everyone's rooms. When he got to the very end of the hallway, there was Jackie. She was sitting in a chair in her room, looking out the window and talking to herself. J.J. sat behind her on the floor, and quietly listened while she talked to herself about various conspiracies. He just hoped she'd bring it up again.

"Stevie Wonder is not blind. This man's songs always have some kind of visual imagery. And why does he regularly spend thousands of dollars to sit court side at professional basketball games? Back in the 70's when Darryl Dawkins used to play basketball, Stevie was the one that gave him the nickname 'Chocolate Thunder.' How did he know that Dawkins was dark skinned? What about the time he took a picture of Michael Jackson when they were at the Motown Museum? And what about when he caught a mic stand that was falling when him and Paul McCartney were performing live?" she questioned.

The conspiracies that J.J. once found interesting were now annoying. They're barely holding his attention. There's only one thing he wants to hear about now. If only there was a way to get her to talk about it. He has so many questions. Regardless, he's prepared to sit all night if he has to.

Hour after hour passed slowly as J.J. didn't move from the floor. He remained focused on Jackie, as she rocked in her chair staring out at the rainy night sky. Every few minutes she belted out a conspiracy more outrageous than the last. After a while, he felt kind of silly. He was coming to the realization that he shouldn't have put so much stock in the ravings of someone that's clearly off. He stood up slowly, trying to fight off the cramping in his legs, and headed for the door.

"A few years after the so called *'King of New York',* Jay Jones left the hospital with a healthy baby boy somehow, even though his died in that hospital, the singer Sapphire committed suicide. She was pregnant, but she never said who the father was. She was in the hospital at the same time his wife was, but she left the hospital with no baby," she said.

He turned around in the doorway and looked at her. He couldn't ignore what she said. He'd heard of Sapphire, but never thought much about her. J.J. didn't know what to say or do. He walked out of her room and let himself back into the padded room. After sliding back the deadbolt locking himself in, he sat on the floor and buried his head in his hands.

Dean was sitting in his house watching tv. The two missing bags of 'items' were sitting on his table out in the open. He was in his underwear, smoking a cigar, smiling with a slice of pizza in his hand. Kora and Redd were looking at him through the window.

"He looks like an even fatter, more disgusting, pedophile version of Chef Boyardee. How'd you allow this loser to take your stuff?" Kora said.

"Shut up Special K. Why don't you just kick the door down, arrest him, and I'll take my stuff back," he said.

"You can't be this crazy. How can I officially arrest somebody and give you the drugs they have? You watch too much television," Kora said.

"Aight, well, whatchu wanna do then?" asked Redd.

"I can't lose my job messing with you fool. You see your stuff on his table, right?"

"Yeah. It's right there," he said, pointing.

"Well get it. Do what you gotta do. I helped you find it. I'm out," Kora says, getting in her car.

As she pulled off, she saw Redd kick Dean's door in and go inside as she sped away. Kora went home and immediately began watching the dvd's. The detail of each one was amazing. For ten hours straight, she intently watched disc after disc, only stopping to use the bathroom. She could literally feel her brain expanding. He didn't miss a single step in any of his many complex processes. Roger was succeeding in posthumously teaching his daughter how to look at things and process everything at a detailed level that most normal people could not understand. She took a break just long enough to heat up some food and got right back to it.

CHAPTER SEVEN

Introducing, The Real Kora Merrit

Jay was signing all the paperwork for J.J.'s release. It took almost forty minutes, but J.J. was finally released to him. He hugged his father but remained silent until they're in the car.

"How do you feel?" asked Jay.

"Dad, we need to talk," J.J. says.

"Ok. What's on your mind son?"

"Did you ever deal with the singer Sapphire?" J.J. asked.

"J.J., I don't really want to…"

"Dad, please. Listen, you're a lot more than just Dad, okay. Please, just tell me the truth. I'm a grown ass man out here making my own mistakes. I would never judge you. I would judge you lying to me though,"

"Okay son, okay. Let me start out by saying this was before I was married, okay. Her and I dated briefly," Jay said.

"Tell me everything Dad," J.J. requested.

"Around the time I got engaged to your mom, Sapphire got pregnant. I was terrified. Soon after that, your mom said she was pregnant. I didn't know what to do. I had a long talk with Sapphire. She wanted to take you on the road with her while she toured. She wanted to have a newborn baby passed around to different drug-heads on her staff while she performed. Bouncing in and out of hotels with seedy people in the business. I told her I was about to retire. I was ready to give you all the time I had. She didn't want to hear it. She wanted you on the concert tour with her. Her preference was to hire a stranger to take care of you for two years while she toured, instead of letting me just take care of my child. I think you know the rest," Jay said.

"Mom had a stillborn and you convinced Sapphire it was hers. Sapphire was my real mother," J.J. said, shaking his head.

"Yes, she was," Jay said.

"Does mom, or Shel, know about this?" asked J.J.

"I'm pretty sure she does. We've never talked about it, but she's a smart woman. I'm pretty sure she knows she didn't birth you, but she'll never say anything about it. For all intent and purposes, Shel is your mother. She's the one that raised you,"

"What happened to Sapphire?" J.J. asked.

She committed suicide," Jay answered.

"Because of me? Because of what happened?"

"No, son. You were at least four years old when she killed herself. By then, she had problems with her record label, abuse allegations with the guy she was dating, and people weren't buying her music anymore. It had nothing to do with you or me. I did what I did to save you from what she was trying to do. I hope you understand that," Jay says.

"I understand Dad. I'm thankful for what you did. Thanks for telling me the truth. I mean, I'm twenty-five now but you know," laughed J.J.

"Yeah Yeah."

After a few days, Kora has watched the dvd's twice. She knew them backwards and forwards. After a complete change of heart, she told the mayor she wouldn't be joining the new unit, and then she reached out to the chief of police and scheduled the detective's exam. There are a lot of rumblings around the department, as the vets are full of hate towards Kora. No one liked how she seemed to get preferential treatment, or the fact that she appeared to have a friendship with the mayor, and the ear of the chief of police.

After posting the highest score the city has ever seen on the detective's exam, 99.3, Kora was allowed to choose which cases she investigated. This doesn't work for anyone at the precinct. The only time she took a break from the dvd's was when she spoke to J.J. on the phone. He couldn't wait to tell her everything about Sapphire being his real mother.

"They're treating this black bitch like she's the Queen of England," Mills said

He's sitting in the parking lot of Rowley Park, eating a slice of pizza. Like most of the department, Mills was completely against all the attention Kora had been getting.

"It's all good though. I sent a couple of the boys to pay her a little visit a while ago. They tuned her up nice. Listen, I gotta go. We'll talk," he boasted.

Mills continued to eat his pizza. It was almost sundown, and the park was packed. He hasn't been assigned a new partner yet. He heard something hit the back of his squad car. Mills got out and walked around to the back of the car to check. There's a dent that clearly had been made from a rock. He looked around but he didn't see anything.

"Savages," he mumbled.

As he walked back to his door, someone hit him in the back of his legs with a bat. Mills dropped to his knees and tried to turn around. Four men with bandanas covering their faces stomped him out savagely. Initially, he tried to get to his weapon, but quickly realized it's in his best interest to just try and cover up his face. Mills could hear all the people in the park cheering loudly as he took a bad beating. After a few minutes, the men all took off running. Mills finally called for backup, but it was too late.

Once the men get a safe distance away, they duck into a basement apartment on Walnut Street. They took their masks off and laughed.

"Tell Merrit we got his ass," Bit says.

The next morning Kora was prepared for the first day of the rest of her life. She put on black boots, tight black pants, tight black shirt, a black headscarf, and a long black trench coat. Her badge was on the front of her hip.

She walked into the precinct with her head held high. Everyone stared at her in disbelief. Kora could feel the hate in many of the officers' hearts, and she didn't care at all. She stopped at her desk and began to gather up a few things. She walked into the captain's office, and he didn't even try to hide his disdain.

"Well, if it isn't the hotshot rookie. What are you supposed to be? You look like a member of the black panthers from the 70's. Anyway, I was told to give you an office. You can take Faisons since he just retired. I was also instructed to let you choose the cases you want to investigate. That should go over well with the rest of the cops here. Here's your detectives' badge. Do you have any questions?" he asked.

"No sir," she replied.

"Good," he said, raising the newspaper over his face.

Kora went over to the missing persons file cabinet. There were hundreds of unworked cases. She didn't even know where to start. She just grabbed five of them and headed over to her new office. The view of the train station put a smile on Kora's face. She took a minute and just watched the people hurrying across Main Street to get to the train. Her new office was great. The large windows beamed with natural light. As she checked the cabinets in her office to make sure they're empty, she heard a voice call her name out. She turned around to see Mills standing in the doorway. He had a black eye and he's using a crutch.

"So, your own office, huh?" he says sarcastically.

"Well, what can I say? Hard work is often rewarded," she replied.

"You know, you may have some of the people here fooled, but not me. I know what kind of person you are. I can't prove it yet, but I know you had those *homeboys* jump me," he said.

"Is that right?" Kora asked.

"That's right. I'm gonna track them down. When I prove you were behind it, you're goin to jail," he threatened.

"You see: that's the difference between me and you. Some goons tried to jump me the other night, but they couldn't. They were soft and they got handled. Interesting thing though, when those good ol' boys were driving away, I noticed they had a bumper sticker with your redneck fish store on it. That's quite a coincidence. I have the plate number though. I hope that truck isn't registered to any of your friends or family," she said sarcastically.

Mills looks down at the ground and frowns. He takes a deep breath. As he tries to walk away, Kora stopped him.

"Not so fast, fatso. This is why you still have a desk in the common area after 20 years. You're just not very bright. I'm not even mad at you Mills. I'm betting the only black woman you knew growing up was Aunt Jemima. We're actual people Mills. It must burn you up to know that I'm smarter than you," she said.

"Are you gonna report me?" he asked.

"No, Mills. You're not worth my time. One day you'll realize that women, even black ones, are just as capable as you good ol' boys. Until you figure that out though, for lunch get me a turkey burger unlimited, Swiss cheese, mayo and ketchup, fries on the side. Thanks. And um, close my door on your way out," she said.

Mills angrily closed the door and struggled down the hallway with his crutch. Kora, grinning, began thumbing through one of the case files. Before she could concentrate, her phone rang. The captain told her there's a suicide a few blocks away, and he'd like his new hotshot detective to take a look and verify that it's a suicide. To her, he just wanted her to mess up so he could say I told you so to all the higher ups. Everyone that walked past her office stared inside in pure disbelief. She threw her jacket back on and headed to the scene.

Melmore Gardens: a quiet street nestled in between the constant traffic of Park Avenue and the imminent danger on William Street. The people who live there have all been there for years. Everyone on the clean block knew and looked out for one another. When she turned onto the block, most of the residents are standing outside, crowded around the police tape, trying to see what's going on. Kora double parked close to the tape and walked up flashing her badge. She ducked under the tape and walked into the house. There's a woman hanging in a doorway. Police were walking around trying to find clues and piece together what happened. Everyone looked up at Kora when she entered the room. Before she could wrap her head around her first crime scene, a man walks up to her:

"Hello, you must be Detective Merrit. They told us they were sending you down. I'm Officer Palmer. It looks like you wasted your time. The victim is Sandra Pane. She was here alone, and no one saw anybody go in or out. She even left a suicide note," he said.

He looked at Kora, but she wasn't not paying him any attention. He and the other officers watched her as she walked around the room looking at everything. Palmer grinned as she went from the body to the china cabinet.

"This is the hero the mayor keeps raving about? What a joke" he whispers to another officer.

"So, I guess we can close this as suicide, right?" he asked.

"This is actually murder," Kora replied.

"Murder? Please, tell us what you found in two minutes that we didn't find in the 2 hours all ten of us have been here investigating," Palmer said as the other cops turned and looked at them.

"First, look at her toenails. The left foot is freshly painted. On her right foot the first two toes are done but the rest aren't. Was she in a rush? Why would she hang herself before she finished painting her toes? The suicide note is written in red ink. I don't see a red pen anywhere. It says that this woman is an English Teacher at the high school. The note says *I didn't think t-h-e-i-r was another way*. Wouldn't an English Teacher know the difference between t-h-e-i-r and t-h-e-r-e? Her pill caddy is labeled according to the days of the week. She took high blood pressure and anti-depressant meds. Why'd she take her pills today if she knew she was gonna take her life?" Kora questions.

"Uh…those are uh…interesting points detective. We…uh…may have …uh…missed a couple of things," Palmer admitted.

"We're all on the same team Officer Palmer. I'm just glad I could help out. Oh, and umm, pick up the husband," she grinned, she couldn't believe how easy it was coming to her.

"Why?" Palmer asked.

"She wasn't wearing her ring; they were having problems. No broken windows, door wasn't forced open. ADT didn't go off. Sweat him a little bit, he'll confess," she stated, heading for the door.

The officers all watch her exit the house with confusion and amazement. She strutted to her car without looking back.

After sitting in her car and taking several deep breaths, Kora realized she even amazed herself. The smile was going from ear to ear.

'Thanks Dad,' she said to herself.

A couple of hours later, when Kora finally got back to the station, her lunch was waiting for her on her desk. After grinning to herself, she checks everything to make sure Mills didn't do anything to it. She tears into her turkey burger while looking out the window. Officer Palmer knocks on her door. She tries to wipe the mayo and ketchup from her face as she signals him to come in.

Detective Merrit, I'm sorry. I didn't mean to interrupt your lunch," he said.

"No problem at all. What can I do for you?" she asked.

"It's actually what you did. The husband confessed after ten minutes of questioning. You were right," he said.

"You got your guy. That's great."

"You got the guy Detective. And to be honest, me and my officers were completely against you coming in the first place. I read the papers, hell, we all did. To read there's a rookie cop jumping all the processes we have to follow pissed a lot of us off. We were already side eyeing you before we even knew you. I just wanted to come by and say that I was wrong about you. You're the real deal Merrit. I hope that in the future if I have trouble with cases I can call on you," he says.

"I appreciate that. Of course, you can. I'm always willing to help out. Don't hesitate to call Officer Palmer,"

"Please, call me Curtis," he says as he puts his hat on and walks out of her office.

"Curtis…" she says low as she watches him walk away.

She turns to her left to see some cops congregated around the captains' office. They're discussing an informant's tip about a big shipment of heroin that's supposed to come into the port tonight. They're going to coordinate with the Newark Police and intercept it.

Redd was in his apartment playing video games with Sascha. They'd already eaten a whole pizza, and now they were running through some chocolate chip cookies. They'd been laughing and joking for a couple of hours. Once again Redd had taken her away from her volatile home situation. They never talked about the drama that went on at her house; they just concentrated on having fun. Sascha could listen to Redd's old stories for hours. He told her countless tales from his life growing up in foster and group homes. Even though her life wasn't the best, Redd's tales often made her appreciate what she had. As much as he wanted a child, Redd didn't want to pay child support for twenty years. He knew that if he ever got his current girlfriend pregnant, she would immediately file with the court. His money was his primary concern, so right now he settled for treating Sascha like his daughter whenever he could.

Sascha had never met her father. He disappeared as soon as he found out about the pregnancy. Her mom worked as a waitress at Fridays. She was doing the best she could. There'd been a parade of men in her life, none of which had been worth anything. The current one, Trevor, might be the worst of all. He's a part time Uber driver and part time weed dealer. If he wasn't putting his hands on her, they were arguing. Redd minded his business, but he was always concerned about Sascha. There was a knock at his door, prompting her to roll her eyes and put down the controller. It' was her mother, and this time she had Trevor with her.

"Hi Redd. It's time for Sascha to come home. You know when she's with you she acts like she doesn't have school," her mom said.

"Yeah, I know. How you doin?" Redd asks.

"She's good," Trevor said, answering for her.

Redd didn't even acknowledge him, he just hugged Sascha as she walked out the door. She looked back at Redd as her and her mom turned to walk away. Trevor didn't move though. He continued staring at Redd.

"What kind of man hangs out with a little girl that isn't his," Trevor asked while rapidly moving his toothpick with his tongue.

"A real one," Redd replied, closing his door.

As he closed his door shaking his head, his phone rang.

"Hey, Special K. What's goin on?" he said

"Do you know anything about a massive heroin shipment coming into the port tonight?"

"Come on now. Nothing comes in or goes out of the port that I don't know about. Yeah, I know it's coming in," he said.

"Well make sure you're not there," Kora warned.

"Damn. Thanks for the tip Special K."

"It's the last one Redd," she said.

"I understand."

Captain Jim Rainer was a traditional idealist that was as outdated as bell-bottom pants for men. He tried his best to run the precinct like an army. He'd been known to try to dock pay for lateness, even going as far as following officers on patrols to make sure they're doing their jobs. Most officers can't stand him, but he doesn't care. A fifty-six-year-old black man that spent 25 years in the military, the captain still makes his bed with hospital corners. He's been known to make officers lives miserable if they get on his bad side. He keeps a mental list of people that annoy him, and now Kora is the object of his ire. He sees her coming in from outside and calls her into his office.

"Yes Captain," she says.

"I hear you're having quite the first day *detective*," he said sarcastically.

"It's going okay I guess," she says.

"Yeah, so I've heard. Merrit, I joined the army at eighteen years old. I went to two wars. In that time, I started as a private. After a couple of years, I became a Private First Class. Soon I became a Specialist, then a Corporal. Finally, I made it to Sergeant, then Staff Sergeant, Master Sergeant, and finally I retired after being promoted to First Sergeant. I came back home and joined the police force. I began as an officer, then an Inspector. I moved up to Sergeant, then Lieutenant, and finally Captain. I never skipped a step along the way. I earned everything I ever got. Do you see where I'm going with this?" he asks.

"No sir, I don't," she said

"I busted my ass for years and never skipped a step. I respected the Army and the force too much to cheat the system to get ahead. I've earned everything I've ever gotten. So, when people like you come to my precinct and skip steps, I get pissed. You're jumping over officers that have put time in. They've given their blood, sweat and tears to this job, and now some young rookie is passing them. It's not fair. I don't like it, and I don't like you. If it was up to me, you would be on Park Avenue and Grove Street crossing kids when school lets out every day. But somehow, one can only guess how, you're in tight with the mayor," he finished, while rolling his eyes.

"What's that supposed to mean?" Kora asked.

"It means no matter what, I'll never be equipped to get in good with the mayor. You don't deserve an office. You don't deserve to be a detective. You're the flavor of the month around here. A six-month cop already promoted to detective, given an office, and the freedom to sashay around here flaunting it in every hardworking cop's face. You're gonna fall Merrit, and when you do, I'm gonna bury you," he said promised.

"Is there anything else captain?" she asked.

"Yeah. Since you were able to just jump right in to being a detective, I'm sure you'd be able to train a junior detective," he grinned.

"I've been a detective for a half a day. Shouldn't I be someone's junior detective?" she questioned.

"You don't need training. You're the superstar. You're gonna show us men how it's done. There's a nerdy useless officer that just passed the detectives exam recently. He's scared of pretty much everything. He's some straight 'A' Princeton grad that's sticking it to his parents by going into law enforcement. I'm pretty sure he's afraid of his own shadow. But he passed the detectives exam, he worked a desk for 2 years, now he's your problem. Get out," he sneered.

She walked out angrily and headed up the hall to her office. Sitting outside her door is a razor thin white guy with thick glasses on. He's typing on an iPad. Kora rolled her eyes and walked into her office, but he jumped up and walked in behind her. She looked him up and down. He can't be taller than five foot four.

"Detective Merrit, I'm Spencer Sitmore. My friends call me Google," he said, extending his hand.

"That's good to know Sitmore. I'm not your friend. Why do they call you that though?" she asks, reaching down to shake his hand.

"I have an eidetic memory," he said.

"Whatever that means," she said, sitting down and opening his file.

"Princeton, 4.0 g.p.a. You graduated high school at the age of 15? Graduated college at 18? Why the hell are you here?" she asked.

"I believe in law enforcement," he responded.

"You're from Alpine? Do you know what Alpine is? I don't understand why you're here," Kora inquired.

"Yes, I know. Alpine is a borough in Bergen County. It's located 15 miles north of Midtown Manhattan. It's the easternmost community in the state of New Jersey. The current population is 1,987, and it's the most expensive zip code in America with a median home price of 4.25 million," he said.

Kora stared at him in disbelief. She sat back in her chair and tried to comprehend what just happened. She smiled uncomfortably and tried to figure out if that was an isolated occurrence.

"So…you went to Princeton. That's a good school. What…uh…what do you know about Princeton?" she asked.

"Founded in 1746 in Elizabeth as the College of New Jersey, Princeton is the fourth oldest Institution of higher education in the United States and one of the nine colonial colleges chartered before the American Revolution. They moved to Newark in 1747, then to its current site nine years later when…"

"I'm gonna stop you there Junior Detective Sitmore. I think I understand why they call you Google. Do you have any friends?"

"I have several acquaintances, but I don't have any friends in the traditional sense," he says.

"Traditional sense?" Kora asked.

"Yes, a friend is defined as a person whom one knows and with whom one has a bond of mutual affection, typically exclusive of sexual or family relations. I have a few people that I know lightly, but they're not close friends, therefore, they are acquaintances," he replied.

"I know what a friend is Sitmore. Are you this way all the time?" she asked.

"I don't understand. What do you mean?" asked Sitmore.

"Never mind. Maybe we can build up to calling you Google. For now, this is the first case I'm working on. It's a missing persons case. The woman's name is Tamica Wrapp. Take a look at the file and see if you find anything. She worked at Foot Locker in Livingston," she says.

He quickly scanned all the papers in the folder while speed-reading every page meticulously. There are fifteen pages in the folder, and within a minute he put it back down on her desk.

"There are no clues in the folder as to Ms. Wrapps' whereabouts," he stated.

"No kidding. Okay Google, where would be the best place to start?" she asked.

"Statistically speaking, the file says that she works six days a week, including every weekend. If that's the case then there is a 72.6 percent chance that her abductor either works with her, or was a customer at her job," he said.

"You might not be as annoying as I expected you to be. Get your coat," she said.

Redd was just getting home after test-driving a new truck. He changes vehicles every six months. A guy that brings home around 8800 dollars a month, he spent most of it on cars, weed, video games, and food. He spends money frivolously and doesn't save much. He's never used his stove and there was never anything in his refrigerator except leftovers. He parked his car and got out, taking a bag of toilet paper from his trunk. He looked over a couple of rows in the lot and saw a guy breaking into a car. The guy was wearing all black and had a garbage bag over his shoulder. He looked over at Redd and immediately got nervous. Hesitantly, he walked over to Redd.

"Hey man. Please don't call the cops," the guy pleaded.

"Don't call the cops? You're breaking into somebody's car that lives in my building!" Redd snapped.

"I know bro, but don't call the cops. If you don't, I'll give you a couple of PlayStation games," the guy said.

"You're trying to bribe me with video games?" Redd asked.

"Um…yeah, that's all I can offer. I mean, unless you want some aroma therapy candles," he said while digging in his trash bag.

"Man, what games you got?" Redd asked.

The man reached into his bag and handed Redd a couple of video games. He accepted them and told the man to leave and never come back. Before he could even get in the house, his phone was ringing. Rashan asked Redd if he wanted to earn some money tonight at the port. Redd told him that he wasn't interested, but Rashan kept upping the amount he's willing to pay him. Redd was adamant about not leaving the house tonight, telling Rashan he had the flu, even though he sounded fine over the phone. After a while Rashan gave up, telling him he'd call him tomorrow, but Redd's refusal to earn an easy ten grand sent up some red flags to him.

That night, Redd stayed in the house, opting to relax and watch basketball. Around 10pm, just like Kora warned, the police raided the port, seized the shipment, and arrested everyone there. Rashan, upset, sat in a police car handcuffed, watching the officers load all of the drugs into a van. He knew he'd not only just lost a ton of money; he was going to be locked up for a while. As Rashan sat in the car pissed, he couldn't stop thinking about how adamant Redd was about not helping with the shipment tonight.

'If I ever find out that Redd knew about this, I'll kill him,' he thought to himself.

Kora and Google arrived at Livingston Mall. One of the most underwhelming malls in the state, it's somehow managed to stay open since 1971. After stopping for a pretzel, they walked over to Foot Locker. After all the customers were out, they questioned three employees: Vanessa, Erica, Angie, and their manager, Mike. Google let Kora do all the talking while he observed. After grabbing buffalo chicken sandwiches, they got back in the car. Kora didn't waste any time opening hers and eating while she started the car.

"Would you like me to drive detective?" Google asked.

"You have a license?" she asked.

"Yes, I do. I've never really driven though. I mean, other than my road test," he admits.

"I see. That's okay, I got it," she said.

"I understand the concept of operating a vehicle though," he says.

"I'm sure you do. Okay, so tell me what you observed in Foot Locker. Let's start with the first girl, Vanessa. I could tell she was smart, sensible, and not a lawbreaker. She has a small child and likes ice cream," Kora grinned.

"How did you get that?" he asked.

"She had a tattoo with a birthdate from a year ago, and her hands were sticky. What did you notice about her?" asks Kora.

"Well, she was going through drama with her boyfriend. Her phone went off several times when you were questioning her. The texts had capital letters and exclamation points. She…"

"I'm gonna stop you right there before you annoy me. I noticed things about the manager that sent up red flags. What about you?" she asked.

"Yes. The employees wouldn't look at him. He's probably assaulting them on the regular. The guy from the video game store walked in and he gave him some sort of head signal and he walked right back out. He's probably illegally trading sneakers for games. He had a cell phone on him and one behind the register."

"Good work Google," she said.

"What about you detective? What did you notice about the manager?" he questioned.

"He was wearing a pair of classic Air Force Ones, just like the person who abducted Tamica Wrapp," she said.

"It's a popular shoe though. That doesn't mean he was the guy,"

"You missed the car key, didn't you? He drives a Camry. I'm willing to bet it's a black one. He's the guy Google," she said.

"I uh…I missed that detective. I don't generally miss things. What's the next step?" he asked.

"We keep an eye on him. Hopefully he leads us to either Tamica Wrapp, or whoever he works for,"

Over the course of the next month, Kora closed several cases with ease. She caught a burglar that had broken into several residences; tracked down a rapist that was stalking women at night, even figured out the identity of a murderer on a cold case. The problem is that she couldn't seem to make a dent in any of her missing persons cases. Even with Googles help, they hit dead end after dead end. She's followed Mike, the Foot Locker manager for three weeks now and gotten nothing.

"So, why do you wear all black every day?" Google asked.

They were sitting in the car outside of Mike the Foot Locker Manager's house. She wasn't ready to give up on him leading her to Tamica Wrapp yet.

"I choose to. You have a problem with black?" she asked, cutting her eyes at him.

"No ma'am. I was just curious."

"It's my favorite color. It looks good on me," she said.

"We've been sitting on this guy for three weeks. Statistically speaking, there's only a 5 percent chance that he would still provide viable information after the first ten days," said Google.

"Well, sometimes you hafta go with your gut and not the numbers,"

"How does that work? I mean, the numbers tell you everything you need to know. Numbers don't lie," he said, confused.

"Do you really think that every situation can be figured out or solved with numbers?" she asks.

"Um, absolutely. We live in a world based on numbers. There's no way that can be…"

She slapped him across the top of his head. He looked over shocked.

"Now what are the odds that I'm going to do that again?" she asked

"Right now, or in general?" he asked confused.

"Right now," she demanded.

"Now that the element of surprise is no longer valid, you wouldn't…"

She quickly popped him across the top of his head again.

"Don't always rely on the numbers. Sometimes you have to use your gut. Your instincts can save your life out here. God, I sound like a seasoned vet," she says.

A dark suv pulls up to Mikes house. He comes outside and a couple of guys hand him a dark bag. He talks to them for a few minutes. They then hand him an envelope.

"How about those numbers now?" she asks.

"I don't understand. This doesn't fit in statistically with anything," he says.

"Yeah. That's usually how it works. Get the plates on the suv," Kora says.

"I already did," he assured her.

"Don't you need to write it down?" she asked.

He looked at her out the corner of his eye, tilting his head back sarcastically.
"Show off," she said.

The suv pulls off and Mike goes in the house. Kora grabbed the radio smiling widely.

"This is Detective Merrit, badge number 02201929. I need a trace on license plate sierra, hotel, echo, garage, radio 8."

"Roger that detective, one moment," a voice says.

"The vehicle is registered to Joe Pascale at 435 Avon Avenue, apt. 101 in Newark," the voice continued.

"Guess we're heading to Newark," Kora says, starting the car.

"Detective, statistically speaking, he just pulled off: there's only an 8% chance of him going directly to his home address.

"Okay Google. As much as I like proving you wrong, I am kinda tired. We can pick this up tomorrow," she said.

After dropping him off at his apartment, she starts thinking about the dvds. She can picture his face plain as day. One of the things Roger said is replaying in her mind.

'If you're my son, you're going to follow everything I say to the letter. You have my instincts and drive, and you probably think like me. If you're my daughter, you're a totally different animal. You have everything I have, and a lot more. Don't suppress your personality to be like me, use it to be better than me. Follow your instincts and remember, I'm just giving you a blueprint. Do things your way and don't ever apologize for it,'

Kora jumped on the parkway and headed to Newark. She parked about a half a block from Joe Pascal's building. There were lot of people outside standing around, talking, riding bikes, and selling drugs. She got out of her car and didn't pay any of the activity going on around her any mind. People stared, but no one said anything to her. She opens the broken front door of the apartment building and makes her way to apartment 101. She knocks on the door and the man she saw stop at Mike the managers house opens it and stares at her.

"What do you want?" he asked with an attitude.

"Information," she replied.

"I don't know anything," he says, trying to close the door.

"I think you do," Kora said forcing her way in.

Joe looked at his handgun that was sitting on a coffee table about six feet away from him. He looked over at Kora, who already had her gun on him. She smiled and nodded toward his table, urging him to try it.

"If you think you can reach it, go ahead and try. But know this, by the time you get to that coffee table, you'll have at least six holes in you," she promised.

He rolled his eyes and sat on his couch. Kora grabbed his gun and removed the clip, making sure there's not one left in the chamber. She placed it back down before going over to close the door.

"I aint telling you shit," he said defiantly.

"Good. I prefer a challenge," Kora smiled.

She pulled an electric stun gun from her back pocket and began to check to make sure it's working. Joe looked like he couldn't care less.

"You think I care about you and your stupid stun gun? I don't. Do what you gotta do, I ain't telling you shit!" He said.

"Cool. Do me a favor, pull your pants down," she requested.

"What?" he asked nervously.

She tucked the stun gun into the back of her waistband and takes out her Glock. She points it directly at his head.

"I said, pull your pants down. While you're at it, take the draws down too. Since you're such a badass, let's see how those little guys react to my stun gun."

"Whoa whoa whoa, hold on a minute now. No need to get violent. What do you want to know?" he asked.

"Tell me about Mike. The guy you met up with a couple of hours ago," she demanded.

"What about him?"

"First, what did you give him when you showed up at his house?" she asked.

"Money,"

"Money for what?" Kora asked.

Joe didn't respond, opting to sit in silence instead. She took out the stun gun and demanded that he pull his pants and underwear down. He stood up to do what she demanded, and instead rushed her. Kora calmly sidestepped and clipped him, causing Joe to hit the ground. His pants were down, and he was on his stomach. She sat on his back and told him not to move, placing the stun gun on his right butt cheek. As he began to struggle to move, she pulled the trigger, shooting volts of electricity into his body through his buttocks. Joe screamed out in pain.

"Let's try it again, why did you give Mike money?" she asked.

"For g-girls. He supplies girls. W-We pay him, and he brings girls that we send all over the world. He's just one supplier," He stammered.

"You're gonna give me a list of all your suppliers, and where you're sending these women," Kora stated.

"I can't give you what I don't have. I'm at the bottom of the totem pole. All I know is that Mike is one of several people that supplies girls. He's the only one I know."

"Okay, so Mike would call you and tell you he has new girls that he's kidnapped. You would pay him. What happens after that? If you're not taking the girls, who is? He has to be dropping them off to someone," she said.

He tried not to answer, so she gave him another dose of electricity. He screamed out in pain, much to her delight.

"After I pay him, someone shows up at his house six hours later and takes the shipment from him," Joe said.

"The girls, you mean.

"Yes, the girls," he said.

"Six hours? We were at his house three hours ago. That means they're still there," Kora realized.

"Let me give you a little warning: this is much bigger than you and I. There are people involved in this that are well above your pay grade. Do you really think a nationwide network can operate quietly without assistance from powerful people?" He asked.

"What do you mean nationwide?" Kora asked.

"I've already said too much. Just lock me up. Please make sure I get solitary confinement," he requested.

Kora puts cuffs on him while deep in thought. After carefully walking him down the stairs and into the back of her car, she called Google and told him to come outside in ten minutes. As the car sped toward his apartment building to scoop him, Joe tried to explain that Kora was making a mistake.

"Detective, you're about to start a war you can't possibly win. If you go and intercept that shipment, you'll win a battle. You have no chance of winning the war," he said.

"Well, we're talking about kidnapping women, right? I'll take the battle," she responded.

She picked up Google who was clearly confused by everything that's happened in the couple of hours since he got out the car. He looked in the backseat and sees a handcuffed Joe, who smiled and nodded at him. He turned back even more confused as Kora explained what has happened.

"So, you're saying that The Foot Locker manager has kidnapped girls at his house right now?" Google said.

"That's what I'm saying. We've got time to recover them before whoever comes to take them away shows up. They'd never be seen again at that point," Kora said.

"But don't you think we should wait outside until the delivery person shows up to take them? We could grab him too," Google stated.

"I don't know. I don't like the idea of leaving kidnapped young women in a house with their abductor any longer than necessary," Kora said.

"Well, how long do we have before the pickup is supposed to happen?" Asked Google.

"At least two hours," she replied.

"Okay, so we call for backup, sweep the house, get the women out fast: no lights and sirens. We arrest the Foot Locker guy and then wait for the delivery guy to come for the girls," Google said.

"That could work," Kora agreed, picking up the two-way radio.

She called for backup at Mike's house. They quickly knocked down the door and arrested him. When Kora and Google walked through the house, they found five women chained to metal pipes in the basement. She looked at them and saw the fear and filth on their faces and bodies. There was a bucket for them to use the bathroom. Google saw Kora's face erode into an angry scowl. As she tried to make her way to Mike, Google stepped in her way and lightly grabbed her. She basically began carrying him toward Mike.

"Let me go," she yelled angrily.

"Detective, there is a 94.8% chance that if I let you go, you'll attack that guy," Google said.

"So what," she agreed.

"So, there's a 68.5% chance that if we move our perimeter back in the next eleven minutes, the person that's going to show up to move those girls won't know we were here. If we grab him without incident, there's a 78.5% chance that he knows more than the Foot Locker guy," he said.

Kora looked at him and stopped struggling. When she did, Googles feet touched the ground again.

"Okay, you can let me go," she said.

They quickly arrested Mike and have officers usher him away. A police van took the women to the nearest hospital to have them checked out. Kora had everyone wait a block away, while her and Google waited in the house for the delivery guy to show up for the girls. Three hours passed and no one showed up to the house. Kora's frustration grew.

"Where is this guy? What the hell is going on?" she growled.

"I don't know. I can't imagine he would be late."

CHAPTER EIGHT

A Meeting 2 Decades in The Making

About an hour later, Kora arrives at her apartment. She takes the mail from her box and smiles at one of her neighbors walking by. She takes the stairs instead of the elevator: an attempt to get in whatever exercise she can. As she walks up to her door, she can hear the television playing inside.

'What the hell?' she thinks to herself, while pulling out her gun.

'It's that damn Redd. I told him to never just show up at my place. He got the nerve to let himself in? I got something for his ass. I'm gonna bust in and act like I think it's an intruder. When I scare the beans out of him, he won't try this again'

Kora bursts through her door and races up to her couch. She's shocked to see a man in a black suit with black shades sitting there. She points the gun at him and instead of reacting, she follows her new training. She takes a deep breath, looks him up and down, and then quickly scans the room. There's another man in a dark suit and shades standing in her kitchen, and a third in the hallway. She puts her gun back in the holster and walks into the kitchen, excuses herself so she can get by the man in there, and takes a Mountain Dew from the refrigerator.

"Okay, so what do the feds want with me?" she asks.

While the men in the kitchen and hallway look confused, the older man on the couch smiles. He takes off his shades and stands.

"You see that fellas? That's how good she is. Most people that come home to find strangers in their place don't react that way. She assessed the situation within a second, and within that second, she figured out we weren't a threat. That's impressive work," the man says.

"I'm glad you're impressed," she says, opening her soda and taking a swig.

"Now tell me why you're here, or I am going to shoot you," she says.

"I'm agent Austin, Detective. I'm sorry for all this. I just had to see it for myself," he grins, removing his shades.

"You had to see what?" asks Kora.

"I've been an agent for 35 years," Austin admits.

"Is that right? You don't look a day over 40," she says.

"Well, I appreciate that detective. You were called to the scene of a Sandra Payne: possible suicide victim. You assessed the situation and in ten minutes ruled it murder. You also said the husband was the killer. In all my years with every agency I've ever worked for, I only knew one person that could do that," Austin says.

"Let me guess: you knew my father?" she asks.

"I did. I was one of the people that got him pardoned by the president when he fled the country. We needed him to track down an international assassin," he says.

"I've heard the story. The Ghost. "I know the rest. He caught her, but she killed him. You brought him back and got him killed," Kora says.

"No, that's not true. Roger Merrit was the best. He wasn't focused. He was always on top of his game, and he always got his man. That last time, he was off. That's why the ghost killed him,"

"Okay, so the ghost killed him. He got her. I know she's in a maximum-security prison somewhere. She hasn't been seen since. What do you want from me?" asks Kora.

"Well, the story you know isn't the complete truth," Austin says.

"What the hell are you talking about?" Kora asks.

"Roger had figured out who the ghost was. The problem was, he had only figured out who one of them was," he says.

"One of them?" she asks.

"We never went public with the information. Turned out, the ghost was four different women. They executed assassinations all over the world for years. They were the one case your dad couldn't close. He figured out who one of them was and thought he had the ghost captured," says Austin

"And then they all executed him," she says, realizing that her father never had a chance at the end.

"Well, even though the one has been behind bars for two decades, the others disappeared and never tried to break her out. They've kept a low profile until about six months ago. They killed a tech mogul in China. A month later they killed an oil tycoon in Abu Dhabi. And just last month they took out a Saudi Prince. All carefully orchestrated, and no one saw anything," Austin says.

"Well, they must be in their mid – fifties by now. I'm sure you'll catch them," says Kora.

"You guys want a soda?" she asks.

"We're on the clock," the agent in her kitchen says.

"I said soda though. Suit yourself," she shrugs, taking another swig.

"Detective, we've been watching you since you were in the academy," Austin says.

"Is that right? And why is that exactly?" she asks.

"We had to know if you had it," he says.

"If I had what?" Kora asks.

"Your father had a gift. The average detective solves 6.2 cases a year. Over the course of a 20-year career that's 124 cases. Roger Merrit solved an average of 6.4 cases per month over the course of 20 years. He solved more cases in a month, than the average detective solved in a year. Over the course of his 20 years, he solved 1,536 cases. Do you know how ridiculous that is? Asks Austin.

"Well, as impressive as that is, I've only solved a few cases. I can guarantee you I'm not the one that's gonna close that many. And his 1,537th case is the one that got him killed. I hope you're not here trying to recruit me to be some super sleuth. I'm just starting out and that wouldn't make sense," she says.

"That's not why we're here," he says.

"Well, you're not drinking, and you didn't bring food, so either tell me what you want, or get out," Kora demands.

We need to catch the other three. They're being paid to eliminate high profile targets again after all these years for one reason: they're the best. Those women are all in their mid to late 50's and they find a way to eliminate targets with full security teams, panic rooms, police escorts, it doesn't matter," Austin says.

"That's sad, but what does it have to do with me? I'm a rookie you know. I just happened to make it to detective. I'm not globetrotting looking for them," she says.

"I don't want you to. We want the one member that is in custody to tell us how to catch the other three. Adriana Jensen; AKA Ursala Grey, AKA Denise Reeves, AKA Christy Long, AKA Maya Ford. She's been locked away in a maximum-security black site for a long time. She was interrogated and tortured for five years. She wouldn't give up anything. We've tried to get her to talk for two decades, but she won't budge. She knows she's never getting out, so we don't have anything to bargain with. She's too smart, too skilled, and feared. After a month, she was running the prison basically. And it's a black site with the worst of the worst! We just didn't have anything to bargain with her until now," he says.

"If you think I'm gonna go talk to one of the bitches that murdered my father, you came a long way for nothing," says Kora.

"I see. Well, maybe this will change your mind," Agent Austin says, placing a file down on her table.

She looks over at him somewhat confused. He nods his head at the file to tell her to open it. She hesitantly puts her soda down and opens the file. There's a picture of her father having dinner with a woman. There's another picture of the woman in a mug shot.

"That woman in the photos is Maya Ford. Your dad was seeing her. It wasn't for long though. Looks like he was seeing her about 23 years ago. How old are you detective?" Austin asks.

She slumps down on the couch, staring at the picture of the two of them at dinner. Her mind begins racing. If this is her truth, she would have preferred to never know.

"You're saying that she's my mother?" asks Kora.

"She's the only person your father saw when he returned from Brazil," says Austin.

"So, you're saying that my mother killed my father? If she's my mother, why have I never been able to find any information on her? I've tried to find out who my mother is for years. I've hired detectives, tried Ancestry, everything. I've only gotten dead ends," she says.

"Your mother is part of the deadliest assassin team we've ever known. Powers higher than you and I have made sure no one would find her," he says.

"So, what do you want from me?" Kora questioned.

"We want you to talk to her. She's always said the only way she would talk is if we brought her daughter to her. I know it's a lot to process, but it's the only way," he said.

"I can't. I'm sorry. I-I can't talk to her," she said sounding sincere.

"You've been searching for this woman your whole life. Why would you not talk to her now?" he asked

"She's a monster,"

"Yes, she is. And we're trying to use her to get three more monsters off the streets," he said.

"I can't help you. I'm sorry," she stated.

"Okay, well, I'm sorry also," he said, placing another file down on the table.

She opens it and saw pictures of Redd working at the port. In the pictures you can see him taking drug shipments and handing them off to various dealers and distributors. She rolled her eyes in disgust.

"You've gotta be kidding me," she said annoyed.

"I wish I was detective. This man, Tyrone Redd Duncan, is a convicted felon. He's been here at your residence as recently as two days ago. He's bringing in drugs from the port every month. You talk to this man regularly. Listen, I know you grew up with him. I don't want to jam anybody up. Talk to your mom, get the information on her three former partners and you never have to see us again. If you don't, Redd is going away for life, and your captain that would love to bust your ass, would be notified that you've been spending time with a felon that you knew was still active in the drug game. I'm sorry, but this is bigger than you and me. We've got a car outside. Don't make this difficult,"

"One conversation: that's all I'm going to do," Kora said, while grabbing her jacket.

"This is a decent apartment. Are you single?" Austin asked.

"If you don't leave me alone," Kora responded.

One of the men takes one of Kora's sodas and puts it in his jacket pocket. She looks at him and shakes her head as they all exit her apartment.

She gets into the car and her mind is racing. After searching for her mother for years, she's not only suddenly on her way to see her, but processing that the woman is evil. They drive for almost an hour, taking all back roads and quiet areas. As familiar as she is with the tri-state area, Kora had no idea where she was. They appeared to pull into a compound. A soldier raised a gate and they drove through to a large, fortified building. There are armed men out front. Austin and Kora got out of the car and walked to the door. A man in a black suit opened it and let them in. Austin led her down a long hallway that seemed like it was never going to end.

"And what exactly do you expect me to get out this woman that I've never met? Kora asked.

"She's smart. Everything she does has a motive. We only have twenty prisoners here, but they're the worst of the worst. Of those twenty prisoners, she's the only woman," Austin informed her.

"Okay, so she's able to survive in a men's facility. It's impressive, but so what?" she said, confused.

"No, you don't get it. She runs this facility. The other inmates all answer to her. Twelve years ago, she killed two men: two full grown convicted mass murderers, at the same time. Apparently, they decided they were gonna dethrone her and take over this place. It took us two weeks to clean up the mess," said Austin.

"That's interesting," Kora replied.

"She's not just tough, she's smart and manipulating. She convinces the others to do whatever she wants: even the workers. We've fired employees for everything from bringing her in cheesesteaks, to assaulting people on the outside for her. She's not gonna volunteer information. She will try to play you," Austin promised.

"And you just want me to go along with that?"

"You're smart. I fully expect you to see through your mothers' games. I'll be right outside. Go right through that blue door. She's inside," Austin says while putting on a headset.

Kora walked into the room and saw a giant officer standing over a woman in a short metal chair. Her two braids ran perfectly down opposite sides of her head. Her oversized prison jumpsuit looked like she had a skydiving suit on. Kora couldn't stop staring at the woman once she walked in. After being locked away at a private prison facility for over twenty years, she has the nerve to be pretty. There are cuts and abrasions all over her hands from multiple fights over the years. Maya, despite being locked away with no hope of ever being released, still beams with an aura of confidence. She looked up at Kora, and almost smiled, but kept her stoic look. She scowled and turned toward the officer standing behind her.

"Get out," Maya told him.

He nods his head and nervously heads to the door.

"And bring me a turkey sandwich," she demanded

"Yes, Ms. Ford," he said, quickly closing the door.

"Kora, it's so good to see you. Please have a seat," Maya instructed.

"I'll stand," Kora responded.

"Suit yourself. You want a sandwich? The turkey is dry, but if you use your imagination, it's just like Boars Head," Maya answered.

"I'm good," Kora responded.

"You look like you have some questions," Maya stated.

"You're kidding right?"

"I haven't seen you since you were a baby. You've grown to become such a beautiful young lady. Ask me anything you want. I'll be happy to answer some of your questions,"

"What do you mean some?" asked Kora.

"I'm in here for five hundred and ten more years. Daughter or not, I can only give you so much for free."

"Why did you kill my father?" She asked

"He got the drop on one of my partners. We had to take him down. I didn't want to, but he was getting closer and closer to us. It had to happen," Maya stated.

"So, you didn't love him?"

"I loved him chasing me. I loved when he would get close, and I would slip away. The closer he got to us, the more turned on I was. He was so good. Did I love him? No. We went on one date and had sex. By the time he figured out who I was, I was putting bullets in him. I cared for him, but business came first, and business was good,"

"Until he took your ass down," Kora said with her arms folded.

"Yeah, he did. He outsmarted me. Even in death, he beat me. Only time I ever lost. Maya admitted, staring into space with a strange look of admiration.

"How did I end up in a foster home," Kora asked.

"Is that a real question? As soon as you were born, they took you away from me and I never saw you again. I was at the top of the F.B.I.'s most wanted list. Once they got their hands on me, they made me disappear."

"Where are the other three?" Kora asked.

"The other three?"

"The other three women you were running with. Where are they and how do I find them?" she questioned.

"Slow down sunshine. I haven't seen you since you came out of me. I got questions of my own," Maya said ".

"I'm not here to answer your questions."

"Well, you gotta cooperate to get cooperation. Tell me about what you're working on in East Orange," Maya requested.

"How do you know where I work? And how do you even know what I do?"

"I traveled the world for years killing folks for money, sweetie. I got people everywhere."

Kora stood with her arms folded, visibly frustrated.

"I got nowhere to go daughter," Maya said, sitting up.

"I'm working on a missing persons problem. Black women are disappearing in my city, and no one knows what's going on. That's what I'm working on," Kora admitted.

"I see. Maybe I can help you with that."

"I don't have five hundred and ten years to wait for your help. I need to figure out what's going on in my city now!"

"Like I said, maybe we can help each other. I got people everywhere. I know it's too late to be your mother, but at least if I can help you out, it'll force you to have to deal with me for a little while," Maya said.

"No. I'm pretty sure someone that's been locked up since I was born can't help me figure out why black women are missing in my town," Kora disagreed.

"Fine. I'm guessing Austin brought you in here. He's been trying to break me for twenty years. I'm not telling you anything. You know that means he's gonna tell you gotta come back here. He's predictable. He's not a bad guy, but a typical suit. He wants my girls so bad, but he'll never catch them,"

"I'm leaving," Kora said, as she turned around and headed for the door.

"Wait a minute. I tell you what: in East Orange there's a crappy fish market on William Street and Munn," Maya said.

"I know the one," Kora responded.

"Go inside and ask for Tron. Tell him Christy sent you. He'll know something about your abductions."

"How do you know that?"

"Because if it happens in East Orange, Tron knows about it," Maya bragged.

"You never lived or worked in East Orange. How could you know people there? How could you have any ties there?" Kora questioned.

"I had to keep an eye on you. If you were there, I was there. I've always kept tabs on you: all those crappy group homes, Manhattan, college, the academy, that loser drug dealer you won't cut ties with. Yeah, I still cast a wide net in here."

Kora was trying to hide it, but she was clearly bothered. Her mother was much more powerful than she expected. Her head was swimming. This was too much to process at once. She felt a bead of sweat roll down her face.

"Did I rattle you my dear? It's okay that your dad is your idol. He closed a lot of cases and put away a lot of bad people. There's something I want you to remember though: I'm the one that killed him. I did what no one else was able to do. I took him off the board," she bragged, while staring into Kora's eyes.

Kora walked out of the room and headed up the hall. She walked past Agent Austin without saying a word. He stood there slightly embarrassed as she power walked by. He continued to look into the room at Maya for a moment before hurrying after Kora.

"I'm sorry, okay? I warned you about how she was though," he said.

"I'm not going to keep talking to that evil bitch," Kora blurted angrily.

"Look, I'm sorry you had to go through that. Unfortunately, you're going to have to keep talking to her until we catch her partners. Otherwise, I have full authority to squeeze you as hard as necessary," Austin admitted.

He opened her car door and watched her get in. He removed his shades and tried his best to show some compassion.

"Look, I don't want to jam you, Kora. I swear I don't. My hands are tied here though. For over twenty years we've interrogated, tortured, threatened, deprived her of every human need except air. She won't break. You're the last card I have to play. I'm really sorry. There are people above my pay grade that are tired of your mother. They're tired of the control she has in that facility and on the streets. You're the first visitor she's had in twenty plus years, how the hell does she still have connections everywhere? They're tired. If I can catch her partners, it could be used to spare her. If she doesn't help us catch them, a lot of important people are gonna say there's no point to keeping her alive. There's no reason for you to care about that, but if we just help each other, we can get through this quickly. Just so you know, even though she always has an agenda, she always asked for you," Austin finished

"You know, I don't like you," Kora said, closing the car door.

"Yeah, I get that a lot," he replied, watching the car drive away.

Google was home feverishly typing on his computer. His apartment had no pictures or art hanging anywhere, not even a television. All he had of any value was an elaborate computer that he built himself. With a tall glass of milk next to him, he continued to research all of the most recent abduction cases in East Orange. He compared the women and tried to find things they have in common. As he looked into every aspect of their lives, he couldn't find anything. As he continues comparing their work and home lives, his phone rang.

Google responded, "Hello".

"Sitmore, this is Captain Rainer,"

"Yes, Captain, good evening," he greeted, sitting up straight.

"Spare me the good boy routine Sitmore. You've been working with Merrit on these missing persons cases, correct?" the captain huffs.

"Yes sir," Google responds.

"What progress has she made to this point?" The captain asked.

"Well, we thought we had a promising lead, but it hasn't really yielded anything concrete,"

"I see. I want to know about any progress made, understand?"

"Yes sir, captain,"

"And let's keep this between us detective. Do you understand?"

"I understand, sir."

"Good. Now, get out of my face." the captain says.

"We're on the phone, sir," Google says sounding confused.

The Chief disconnects the call, leaving Google baffled. He shakes his head and continues to work on his computer.

Redd is coming out of his usual soul food spot on 4th Avenue. He hits the alarm on his vehicle and hears someone call his name. Turning around, he sees Rashan walking up to him. After putting his food in the drivers' seat, Redd turns around to face him.

"What's the word, Rashan? Redd asked.

"You tell me, bro. That night I tried to get you to earn a little extra loot, we ended up gettin' busted. Cops knew what was up and rolled on us," Rashan said, clearly annoyed.

"That's messed up bro. I know you was pissed," Redd responded.

"Pissed ain't the word. I remember I kept trying to get you to work with us that night, but you wasn't hearin' it," Rashan went on, staring hard at Redd.

"Yeah, I couldn't do it that night, bro. I guess I was lucky."

"Yeah, lucky," Rashan repeated the phrase, his voice dripping with sarcasm.

"Well, I got hot soul food, bro. I'm glad you're out though. Hit me up next time there's a job. You know I'm down," Redd told him.

"Aight. Redd,"

Redd opened his car door and moved his food over to get in. Just before he closed the door, Rashan stopped him again:

“Hey Redd, you still tight with that chick that’s a cop?”

“We grew up together. We’ll always be cool, why?” He asked.

“No reason. I’ll talk to you later bro,” Rashan murmured, walking off.

Redd drove away, well aware that he was going to have to deal with Rashan at some point.

As Google felt his eyes getting heavy, he turned off his computer and got ready to go to bed. He’d started turning the lights off when he heard a knock at his door. It’s the first time he’s ever heard a knock at his door at night. Google walked over and opened the door just enough to see through to the other side. As soon as he can see that it’s Kora, she pushed the door open and walked into his apartment.

“Detective Merrit? Well, sure, come in,” he said, confused.

“Google, I’ve had a hell of a day. I got a lot to bounce off of you. I may have a lead for us. I saw my mother, these agents came to my house, and I… are you wearing Batman Pajamas?” Kora asked, looking him up and down.

“My mom bought them for me,” he admitted.

“Of course she did. Wait a minute, are you getting ready to go to bed?” She asked.

"Well, yes actually. I try to get nine to ten hours of sleep every night."

"It's 9 o'clock Google. Get dressed. We gotta get over to the fish market before they close."

"I – um – okay, I will do that," he says, going into his bedroom to put clothes on.

Kora looked around his living room and was surprised to see that there is nothing on the walls. She scanned the space and saw that he literally had nothing but a computer and a router. She shook her head and walked into his kitchen and opened his refrigerator. Much to her surprise, there's a six-pack of Mountain Dew. Smiling, she snapped a bottle out of the plastic and opened it. As she began to drink, Kora continued to look around the room.

"There they are," she said, finding a bag of potato chips.

Her phone rang, echoing throughout the empty apartment.

"Merrit," she answered.

"Hey, Detective, it's Curtis. Curtis Palmer from the …"

"Yes, Officer Palmer, I remember. What can I do for you?" She asked.

"I wanted to know if you'd like to get dinner on Friday?" He questioned.

"That sounds like fun, but I don't really have time for fun right now. I'm knee deep in

Abduction cases. Somebody has to work them," Kora said.

"Well, maybe I can help. Maybe we can go through what you got: over drinks?" He suggested.

"As nice as that sounds, I'm not gonna have fun and drinks while young black women are being taken," Kora answered.

"I get that. Maybe another time then?" He asked refusing to take no for an answer.

"Absolutely. I would like that," she said, clicking him off the phone.

As she really began to get into her snack, Google came out of the bedroom.

"I helped myself. I didn't think you would mind," Kora explained as she tossed a chip into her mouth.

"Of course not Detective. I don't drink Mountain Dew," Google stated.

"Then why do you have a six pack in your fridge?"

"Since we've been paired up, I've seen you drink thirty-seven Mountain Dew sodas. I've also seen you stop working at the correct time only twice. There was an 87% chance that at some point you would come here after hours for a work-related inquiry. The proper thing to do was to stock your preferred beverage of choice," Google stated sounding like his namesake.

"Whatever, let's go," Kora blew him off with a shrug.

Thirty years ago there was a fish spot on the corner of William Street and Munn Avenue known as Blackwells. They were known for their four-dollar whiting sandwich that would have at least twenty full pieces of fish in between two slices of bread: doused in hot sauce. The line would be around the block every day. It was a staple of East Orange: if you lived in town, you had Blackwells once a week.

After they sold their business and moved out of town, the new owners didn't keep the same level of quality people had grown accustomed to. Today, it's a low-quality spot where you could smell the old grease from up the block. There are no more long lines, or big sandwiches. The owner Chuck Boogie Daniels is a large intimidating man. He keeps a gun on his hip while he fries his fish behind the counter. In the back of the small store there's an old rickety table and two old chairs. There's an old guy sitting there that looks like he's had an above average amount of life experiences. His long grey beard is almost resting on the table. He has at least ten gold bracelets on his wrist, with a pair of young boy jeans. Kora and Google walk in, and Boogie stops scooping fish to look them up and down.

"If y'all ain't eatin, get out," Boogie says loudly.

"We're cops," Kora informed him.

"I don't care. It's my business: my rules. You're not in uniform. You're either patrons or you gotta go," he said.

"Give me two whiting sandwiches to go," Kora said, putting a twenty on the counter.

"Boogie takes the twenty with an attitude and goes back to frying. They walked up to the man sitting in the back of the store. He tried to act like he didn't see them. He has his phone out, and he's looking down.

"Are you Tron?" Kora asked.

"I didn't do anything," he responded.

"I didn't say you did,"

"Then what do you want?" Tron asked nervously.

"I need some information. What do you know about the missing women in this town?"

"I don't know anything about that," he responded defensively.

"Tron, I know you know something. If you tell me what you know, we'll leave you alone. If you don't, it's gonna get a little tricky," Kora stated looking him dead in the eye.

"I got no problem with tricky, lady. I'll record whatever you do. I know my rights. Like I said, I don't know anything.

"Fine, we'll go then. Come on Google," she said, walking toward the door.

She grabbed her bag of sandwiches off the counter and stood in the doorway.

"Christy was the one that sent me," she said as they walked out.

Kora saw some kids sitting outside the fish market visibly hungry. She handed them the bag of sandwiches and their faces lit up. They cheered as they tore the bag open and went to work on the fish. Tron came barreling out of the store after them.

"Why didn't you just say that Christy sent you?" He demanded.

"I didn't think I had to," Kora shrugged.

"Listen, all I know is that the 10th Street Hoods are involved. They grab a woman every week and give them to someone. That's all I know, I swear," he pleaded.

"Thanks Tron. That wasn't so hard, was it?" Kora asked.

"Please tell Christy I told you everything I know," Tron begged.

"I will," Kora promised.

"Geez, who's Christy? That guy sure was scared of her," Google said, while watching Tron walk back into the store.

"That would be my mother," Kora admitted.

"Huh?" Google said dumbfounded.

"I guess I better fill you in," Kora answered, as they walk back to the car.

Redd got out of his truck and walked into his place. His apartment smelled like weed and air freshener. After putting his keys down, he looked out the window. Slumping down on his couch, Redd grabbed his television remote and kicked his sneakers off. Before he could get too comfortable, there was a knock at his door. He walked over and peeked out of the peephole and didn't see anything. That always made him smile because it meant little Sascha was standing on the other side. He opened the door and she yelled his name, hugging him.

CHAPTER NINE

Swimming with a Gator

In the dark car parked on 10th Street in East Orange, Kora and Google sit and watch the home of Gator Simms, the leader of the 10th Street Hoods. They've been sitting outside for a couple of hours, and Google is fighting to stay awake.

"Do you have a plan?" he asked, while letting out a yawn.

"Absolutely. We're going to grab him, torture him, and interrogate him until he tells us what we want to know," Kora stated.

"I'm sorry what?"

"You heard me, Google. This is bigger than us. If we're going to get answers, we gotta get a little dirty," she said.

"We could lose our jobs. You're talking about breaking protocols, no warrants, no chain of command," Google said nervously.

"You gotta relax. I have a plan," she said, taking out a couple of ski – masks.

"Well, that's reassuring," he said, slumping down in his seat.

There were two armed men on the first floor of Gator's house. One was playing a video game, and one was texting. The lights go out and they look around confused. As they go to get up from the couch, a masked Kora and Google point guns at them.

"Sit back down," Kora said, disguising her voice.
"Tie em' both up," she ordered

On the top floor of the house, Gator was in bed asleep. There were at least ten guns in his room, along with multiple knives. He always slept on his back while slightly elevated, facing the door. He's usually a notoriously light sleeper: but today, he's knocked out. A hand went over his mouth, and his eyes widened instantly. He struggled and tried to move, but saw a gun pointed in his face. He looked into the faces of the ski-masked Kora and Google and decided to struggle anyway. Kora hit him in the head with her gun and he instantly passed out. Google put his hands on his head in disappointment.

"Oh, stop being a baby. Carry him down the stairs and put him in the car," Kora demanded.

"You're kidding right? This man is at least two hundred and fifty pounds. He must be six foot four. I can't carry him," Google stated.

"You should be ashamed of yourself. I'll carry him," Kora said.

She lifted him out of the bed and fireman carried him down the stairs. Google couldn't hide his embarrassment. They put him in the car and sped off. If you go all the way down Orange Street, there are horse stables in Newark where the cops keep their horses. They tied Gator to the back of one of the stables and threw a bucket of water on him, waking him up.

"What the hell is this? He asked.

"Shut up. You're gonna answer our questions," Kora said in a raspy voice.

"I ain't gonna tell you shit," Gator said trying to sound tough.

Kora pulled his pants and underwear down. His mood instantly changed to fear. She went over to a light and broke it, putting the wires together and making a spark. As she walked towards him with the wires in her hands, he instantly had a change of heart.

"Please don't touch me with that! What do you want to know?" Gator asked.

"You and your goons abduct women every week. Who are you passing off them off to?" Kora asked.

"We never see him. They call him John Doe. We grab a bitch, and…"

"Try again!" Kora yelled, putting the wires together and making a spark.

"We grab a chick, and we drop them off at a different spot. John Doe calls us. The van pulls up, we open the back doors, and our money is in there. We put the bi…chick in, and we leave. He calls to make sure we got a shipment, and then it's on," Gator explained.

"What number does John Doe call you from?" Kora questioned.

"A blocked number. I don't ask questions. As long as my money is right, we don't have any issues," Gator said.

"When is the next drop off?" she asked.

"Tomorrow at midnight. Ampere Parkway," he told her.

They turned to leave. Before they are out of sight, they heard Gator.

"Hey officers. You'll never catch that guy. Someone big is bankrolling the operation. They're smart," He laughed.

"What makes you think we're cops?" asked Kora.

"Only cops would grab me out of my house without hurting my guards or me. I know you got a job you're trying to do, and I respect that, but at the same time, you're trying to take money out my pocket. John Doe is a legend in the hood. Whoever he is, he got a real team behind him. If I had to guess, with all the cash we bring in, some of your brothers must know the deal," Gator warned.

They got in the car and sped away, taking off their ski masks.

"Based on the information we have; Gator will warn John Doe about the events of this evening. I estimate we have a two percent chance of catching John Doe if we show up to that meet," Google said.

"Well, what do you want me to do Google? We can't let them keep abducting these women and sending them off to God knows where to do God knows what," she angrily said.

"Well, you've already made me a criminal. We kidnapped a gang leader tonight. If this John Doe is really connected, we're never going to catch him by showing up to an exchange,"

"Okay, what do you suggest Google?" she asked.

"Well, I'm a five-foot five white guy and you're a local hero. We can't go undercover to try and infiltrate these guys," he laughs.

"And we don't have that much time. I need to know where they're sending these women after they grab them. There's a ton of missing person's cases in the office. Most of them are young black women of course. I want them found! I want this madness over!" Kora blasts.

"I'm with you detective. I want to put an end to it also. There's a high probability that they're shipping these women out of the country. If we catch John Doe somehow, unless we're leaving the country, we'll never find the women that are already missing. Unfortunately, some of them may be dead as well,"

"You're always a ray of sunshine Google. First, we worry about stopping the abductions that are happening, and then we try to track down the cold cases. If it takes us out of the country, so be it," said Kora.

Her phone rings several times as she tries to decide whether or not to answer.

"Merrit," she answered.

"Hello daughter. How are you this evening?" Maya asks.

"How do you have this number? How are you calling me?" asks Kora.

"I can't have phone privileges? Even prisoners get to make a call," she says.

"It's almost midnight. You're calling me from your prison cell. I'm gonna let Agent Austin know that you have a cell phone in there," Kora promises.

"That's a waste of time, and you know it. I think they've taken over a hundred phones from me in twenty years. What are you doing?" Maya asks.

"No. You don't get to call me and ask questions. I don't have anything to say to you. Don't call this number again," says Kora.

"Okay, wait a minute. I just want to know how your search is going," Maya says.

"I'm not gonna talk to you about official police business," Kora says.

"You're just like he was: so professional,"

"Don't do that. You don't get to talk about him!" Kora blasts, raising her voice.

"And there's the difference: those raw emotions. Your father always kept them in check. That's why he was so good," says Maya.

"He was who he was, and I'm who I am. Are you finished? I have to go," says Kora.

"Okay fine. How are you gonna catch John Doe without my help though?" Maya asks.

"How the hell do you know about that?"

"Never mind that. I can help you get him, but you gotta do something for me," offers Maya.

"I don't know how you know so much, but there's nothing I can do for you. Whatchu want me to recommend that they shave a hundred years off your sentence?" Kora asks.

"Don't make jokes with me little girl. I let you slide because you're my daughter, but don't be fooled, I am not someone you ever want to piss off,"

"Miss me with all that tough talk. You may have people feeding you information, but you don't have power on the outside. You want to deal with me so bad, my slick mouth is part of the deal," Kora says.

"When you're ready to address me with the respect I demand, you know how to find me. Until then, go ahead and chase your tail trying to find John Doe. Good night: and good night Google," says Maya.

"Good night," Google says, looking extremely confused.

After another week, two more young black women have disappeared in East Orange. Kora hasn't come any closer to catching John Doe. She's visibly frustrated every day and trying her best not to take it out on her junior detective partner. Every day that she hits a dead end, she becomes angrier and more annoyed. Finally, she wakes up for work, and instead of doing her hair; she walks into the station with a big natural Afro. The disgust on her fellow white officers faces is obvious. Her captain just shakes his head every time he walks past her office door. As Kora sits at her desk trying to figure out what she's missing, Google walks in.

"Detective Merrit. That's an interesting hair style," he observed.

"Don't you know you're never supposed to comment on a black woman's hair?" Kora warned.

"Oh, I'm sorry detective. I didn't mean anything by…"

"Relax Google. I'm just giving you a hard time. What do you got?" Merritt asked.

"Well, I was up late last night and did some digging," he started.

"What's late for you Google? You stayed up til ten?" Laughed Kora.

"Ten thirty actually. I accessed the FBI and CIA's encrypted databases and searched for everything they had on your mother," Google informed her.

"And…?"

"She's been at that super max prison for a long time," he replied.

"I already knew that Google," Kora said sounding emotionless.

"Okay, did you know that her father, your grandfather, is Damien Morris?" Google asked.

"Who's that?" She asked.

"Damien Morris is a multi-millionaire weapons dealer, money launderer, international thief, and broker of every high-end illegal deal for the last forty years. He's known and feared all over the world. Morris was number one on the FBI's most wanted list," he stated.

"Was?"

"He was taken into custody two weeks ago," Google responded.

"Eventually everyone gets caught," Kora stated matter of factly.

"Yeah, well not this guy. Damien Morris surrendered and turned himself in to FBI custody. They had no idea where he was."

"Okay, Google. You have my attention. Where are they holding my …grandfather," she asked

"That I couldn't find. You'll have to ask Agent Austin.

"Well, we can revisit that after we get some of these missing persons cases closed," Kora said

"That's my point, Detective. This man is one of the most powerful people in the world. He's probably had a hand in hundreds of killings. This missing persons epidemic here is clearly a small part of some big business. I'm guessing Mr. Morris knows about anything that's big in terms of illegal business," Google finished.

"I appreciate your opinion: but coming in contact with one insane parent is more than enough for me right now. We can figure this out on our own."

"Okay, I'm with you, you know that. How though? Google quizzed.

"If this is some big operation, somebody's getting rich. We just need to find the money," Kora said thinking out loud.

Kora's cell phone rang and she answered it hesitantly. Google watched the intensity on her face as he tried to figure out what the discussion was about. As soon as she gets off the phone, Kora accelerates toward the precinct.

"Uh....what happened Detective?" He asked.

"A guy was just picked up behind Elmwood Park trying to abduct a woman. They've got him at the precinct. We're finally gonna get our answers!" She promised.

Within five minutes, Kora and Google arrive at the precinct. She makes her way quickly through the hall as he struggles to keep up with her. After turning a corner and seeing an officer at the water cooler, she slaps the cup of water out his hand.

"What the hell?" The officer said sounding slightly confused.

"Where's the guy that was brought in for the attempted kidnapping?" Kora questioned.

"Interrogation room two," he replied.

She stormed down the hall and the captain was standing outside the large window of Interrogation room two. She could see the young black man sitting in the room looking nervous. She reached for the doorknob and the captain blocked the door.

"Where the hell do you think you're going?" The captain asked.

"To get answers. He's gonna tell me who he works for, who the people he works for, work for, where they're taking these kidnapped girls, everything," she said.

"Well, I have other detectives that can extract that information. You're not going in there. Why don't you go to your office and wait? We'll call you if we get something," the captain stated and stared at Kora.

Google looked down and away nervously. He could see the fire in Kora's eyes, and he was not sure not what he should do.

"Captain, if I may?" He began.

"I think we…"

"I don't care what you think, Sitmore. The two of you need to go away," The captain dismissed them.

"You know, usually I let you or the other testosterone – challenged, out of touch, insecure sexists feel like you run this place. I don't have time today to play along. Your ego is gonna hafta get bruised today. I'm going in there to question that perp," Kora shot back.

"Oh shit," Google whispered under his breath, while looking away.

"Who the hell do you think you're talking to? I'm the captain here! I run this place!" He growled.

"On paper you do. Let me and my partner go in there and question him, or I'm gonna call the mayor and tell him you're not taking me seriously again," Kora threatened.

The captain stood silently for a few seconds while staring at Kora with pure hate and disgust. He started to say something, but he couldn't seem to form words. He angrily picked up his folders from the table and walked away, leaving the door unguarded.

"Let's go Google," Kora encouraged, opening the door.

"That was…impressive," Google stated smiling.

Outside the precinct, five black Chevy Tahoes pulled up in front of the precinct. All four doors opened on each vehicle, and out-stepped men and women with the same dark blue F.B.I. jackets on. All twenty of them walked up the steps and into the precinct. At the front door, Captain Rainer stood looking slightly confused.

"What is this?" He asked.

"Dev Warren, F.B.I. You have a suspect in custody by the name of Francis Smith. We're here to take him into custody.

We also need any and all paperwork you have on him and any person or persons, events, and connecting cases to him," the agent said, while handing the captain a warrant.

"What did this guy do? Why is he on your list?" the captain asked.

"That's classified. We'll go through your files ourselves," he says, signaling the other agents to start going through all the precincts files.

"And where is Smith?" He asked.

"He's being interrogated by a couple of my detectives," the captain responded, grinning.

"Stop that interrogation now! Take me to Smith!" Agent Warren demanded.

Inside the interrogation room, Kora and Google had no idea what was going on outside. They're sitting with Francis Smith, the man that was caught trying to abduct a young black woman. He appeared nervous and didn't really want to talk. Every time Kora asked him a question, he just sat quietly.

"Listen, whoever you're afraid of, I can protect you," Kora told him.

"You're a woman. How could you protect me?" Francis asked.

"Seriously? You're better off with me than anybody else here, believe me," she assured him.

"Well, I ain't talkin'. Get me a lawyer," he said.

"I tell you what: how about I just let you walk out of here?" Kora offered.

"What are you talking about?" Francis asked.

"Yes Detective, what are you talking about?". Google chimed in.

"You don't need a lawyer, you can go. Go ahead, walk right out that door," Kora informed the suspect.

Francis stood up confused, pushed his chair in, and headed for the door.

"When you leave, we'll let the streets know we released you because you cooperated," she smiled.

"Now wait a minute! I didn't tell you anything," Francis stuttered angrily.

"No, you didn't. But everyone will think you did when they see you on the street an hour after you were arrested. And I'm definitely gonna tell my contacts that you talked," the officer promised.

"Okay, listen, you gotta protect me. You don't understand. I'm a dead man for getting busted. This whole operation has to be stealth. I want a name change and a new life. Send me somewhere quiet, where I can run through white soccer moms and smoke meat in my backyard," Francis begged.

"Fine, talk!", Kora yells, jumping up and angrily banging on the desk.

"Okay, okay. The operation is run by …"

The door bursts open and Agent warren came in, along with a couple other FBI agents and the captain.

"What the hell?!" Kora blasted.

"Detective Merrit, this is FBI Agent Dev Warren. They have a warrant for this guy and every piece of paperwork associated with him. Sorry, but it's legit. You have to turn him over to them," the captain stated.

"The hell I do! He's about to talk," Kora informed her boss.

"Stand down Detective. We're outranked here. There's nothing we can do," the captain warned.

Kora slumped down in her chair, frustrated and defeated. As close as she was to getting answers, she'd hit another dead end. The F.B.I. agents took Francis out of his chair and put him in handcuffs. He looked at Kora and shook his head before being whisked out the door. She banged her hand on the desk violently, then a second time. Before she could go for a third, Google caught her hand.

"You're going to hurt yourself," he said.

"So what. These young black women are out here being hurt every day. No one cares!" Kora fumed.

"You do though. And I do…" he assured.

"You're doing your job Google. I respect that, but don't get it confused. You're a white man. You don't understand the struggles or the hell that a black woman or any woman goes through day in and day out just to be heard," she told him.

"You may be right about that Detective. But, I'm guessing it takes ears to be heard. You have mine. Instead of pushing me away, build off of that," Google stated.

"Fine," Kora muttered, looking him up and down.

"What do you suggest we do next?" She quizzed.

"Well, The FBI clearly has an interest in this situation. Let's find out why they wanted Francis so bad," Google suggested.

Redd was driving through the city blasting his music. He was playing music, texting, eating potato chips, and eyeballing different women that walked by. He pulled up to a red light on Walnut Street and kept texting. A young woman with short shorts walked past his vehicle and into the corner store, keeping Redd's attention the whole time. After lightly honking the horn, she doesn't respond. As the light changes, a car quickly pulls in front of him. Confused, he looks on his side and sees another vehicle that is parallel to him. The passenger in the car lifts a gun and fires it at Redd several times. He quickly puts his seat all the way down as the bullets go whizzing through his car, hitting the dashboard and passenger window. Feeling intense heat on his arm, Redd knows he's been hit. With the seat all the way down, there's the sounds of people screaming and running. Redd struggles to try to reach his glove compartment without lifting his head over the opening of the drivers' side window. He heard a couple more shots and can feel the impact of them hitting his truck. As Redd rolled over to his side to grab his gun from the glove compartment, he can hear the sound of police sirens. The feet sound like they're running away. As Redd let out a sigh of relief, he looked over to see how bad his arm is. It's covered in blood and the pain was setting in. He tried to move it, but the intense pain made him dizzy. All he could do was wait for the police and ambulance to arrive.

Kora was in her office throwing boxes around and trying to regain her composure. Google had been trying to calm her down to no avail. She slumped at her desk and slapped a stack of papers to the floor. Full of frustration, Kora buried her head in her hands. Her phone rang but she didn't move.

"You want me to get that?" Google asked.
"Would you?" Kora responded and gave him a half smile.

"This is Detective Merrit's phone," Google stated into the receiver.

"It's Agent Austin. I'll put it on speaker," Google said, as he watched Merrit's reaction.

"What do you want Austin?" Kora asked.

"It's time for you to have another conversation with her. We'll pick you up tomorrow. Does that work for you?" He asked.

"If I say no, does it matter?" Kora shot back.

"No, it doesn't. I'm sorry. The car will be at your house tomorrow at 8am," he said, hanging up.

"I need to shoot somebody," Kora joked.

"Uh, I'm sorry?" Google looked away.

“Yeah, I’m gonna have to kill some folks tonight,”.

“Detective, what are you saying?”

“I’m talking about Call of Duty, Google,” she laughed.

“You play?” He asks excitedly.

“I do. Not as often as I used to, but every now and then I get out there and let off some steam,” Kora told him.

“Wow, I play every day. You have to tell me your gamer tag so I can look you up and game with you sometimes!” Google said sounding excited.

“Black Law and Order Boss Bitch 99,” Kora said with a slight smirk.

“Ummm…. okay. I’ll uh, look you up next time I’m on.

Kora’s cell phone rang. She considered not answering but finally decided to. She was listening intensely. Google could tell something was wrong. She raced out of the room to her car and sped away.

“How’s the search going Sitmore?” The captain asked, walking into Kora’s office.

“Oh, uh…well, we thought we were about to have a breakthrough with Francis Smith. The F.B.I. had other plans,” Google told the captain.

“Yeah, I guess they did. I told you to keep me updated on how your investigation is going. Keep me updated means when you think you have a breakthrough, you tell me about it. I don’t want to know about it after you have said suspect in custody that you're expecting to give you vital information. Do you understand?" the captain asked

"Yes sir." Google answered.

East Orange General Hospital. This 211- bed facility was the only fully accredited, acute care hospital in Essex County. It's a staple of city that has stood tall for years. Kora burst through the front doors and rushed to the stairs. Her haste caused people in the hallway to stop and stare. She walked into room 3301 and sighed an annoying sigh of relief. There was Redd, sitting up in the bed, with a doctor stitching up his arm.

"What the hell happened?" She asked, full of concern.

"They tried to get me, Special K. Rolled up at the light and just started squeezin' off. I don't know how I'm alive," Red informed her.

"Do you know who did this?" Kora grilled him.

"I've got a few ideas. I'm gonna handle this. You a good guy now, you ain't gotta get your hands dirty."

"Shut up, Redd. Don't start with that tough guy talk," she responded.

"Somebody tried to take me out. They almost got me, Special K. Your boy was almost outta here," Redd said excitedly.

"So let me handle it. Who do you think it was?" Kora continued to question.

"I don't know. I'm gonna find out though," Redd promised.

"Just don't do anything stupid. Let me handle it. I gotta go Redd. I'll check on you tomorrow," Kora stated as she moved toward the door.

"Aight."

Kora walked out of Redd's room and made her way down the stairs to the lobby of the hospital. She walked out the front door and headed to the street. A black SUV pulled in front of her, and the passenger side door opened. A man in a black suit with shades stepped out and looked at her.

"Ms. Merrit," he said, opening the back door.

Kora spotted Agent Austin sitting in the back smiling at her.

"This some bullshit," she mumbled under her breath, while climbing into the back of the suv.

"Good to see you too, Kora," Austin says flippantly.

"Save it. I'm not gonna keep doin this for you," Kora huffed.

"Of course not. I just need you to talk to her until I get what I need," Austin replied.

"Anyway, let me ask you something. I had a lead on a case I was working, and your people showed up and took my perp away," she said.

"Sorry to hear that. He must've been important to something bigger than your case," Austin answered.

"I don't think there's anything bigger than dozens of missing young black women," she said angrily.

"Of course not. I didn't mean to sound insensitive," he corrected.

"I wanted to punch that FBI Agent right in his face," Kora stated flatly.

"What was his name?" Austin questioned.

"Agent Dev Warren. Him and a bunch of your people raided our office, took every lead we had and swiped our perp before he could talk. "

"I don't know him. Gordon, Reed, either one of you know Agent Dev Warren?" he asked the men up front.

"No sir," they both replied.

"Let me check something," Austin said.

He opened a laptop and began to type. He looked confused and hit a few more keys. He looked over at Kora baffled.

"Ummm, you're not gonna believe this, but we don't have an FBI Agent named Dev Warren anywhere in the department," Austin remarked.

"What the hell are you talking about?" Kora fumed.

"I'm serious. I don't know who came to your department, but they weren't F.B.I."

"How is that possible Austin? There were at least twenty agents. Maybe he's just not in your system," she said grasping at straws.

"If he works for the FBI, he's in this system," Austin assured her.

"What the hell is going on?" She asked confused.

"I don't know. Sounds like whatever the case is you're working on, somebody's going through a lot of trouble to keep you in the dark.

"I gotta get back to my computer Austin. Let's get this over with quickly," she demanded.

"Sure, no problem. And umm, how about dinner tonight," he asked.

"I don't eat dinner. I just want this done," she said.

A few minutes later, Kora walks into the small room and sees Maya sitting and eating a sandwich. The giant guard standing over her looks nervous as he never takes his eyes off of her. She puts her sandwich down and gives Kora a scowl.

"Hello Daughter," she says emotionlessly.

"Do you know the whereabouts of the other three women you used to run with?" Kora asks.

"Wow, I can't get a hello or nothing," Maya says.

"I just need you to give up this information so I can stop coming here. I'm busy and I have cases to close," she says impatiently.

"You searched for me your whole life. How can you find me and say you don't want to see me? That doesn't make sense," Maya says, confused.

"Where are you old partners?" Kora asks.

"Are you still stressing over those abductions?" Maya asks.

"Do you know where the other women are?" asks Kora.

"Let me tell you something honey: black women have been getting taken since I was out. No one gives a damn. The racist cops in charge would work a missing prostitute case harder than a missing sista.' And you aint in charge sweetie," Maya says.

"Well, I'm on it. I'm doing what I can to stop it. I'm trying to make a difference," Kora says angrily.

"That's cute. You're just one person against the world Kora. Those are impossible odds," she says.

"If you think like that, you've already lost," Kora says, standing up.

"This is a waste of time Austin. She's not gonna tell us anything," she continues.

"That attitude: where do you get it from?" Maya asks.

"I won't be coming back here," Kora promises.

"You will, actually. You need me. I guess you don't realize it yet," says Maya.

"Right, you take care," Kora says, opening the door.

"Hey Daughter, I know you're a badass. You think you're invincible. The same way I thought I was. When reality got to me, look where it put me. I've been in here over twenty years,"

"Because you were a bad person. You killed people. You chose your path, I'm choosing mine," Kora says.

"I know there's some of me in there somewhere. I can tell. You'll come back to me on your own. Until you do, I would suggest you look very close to you Dear," Maya says.

Kora walks out the door frustrated.

"That's where your biggest enemy always is!" Maya yells as Kora hurries down the hallway.

At the hospital, Redd is laying down with his arm bandaged and elevated. The police just questioned him and left: protocol after a shooting victim is hospitalized. He's drinking iced tea and watching Jerry Springer, finally calming down from the events of earlier. Rashan walks in the room and Redd can't believe he has the nerve to stroll into his room after the shooting. He sits up as quickly as he can, trying not to show weakness as the pain shoots through his arm. Rashan stares at him with a blank expression. The two look at each other awkwardly in complete silence for several seconds. Rashan pulls out a small silver handgun and points it at Redd. With nowhere to go, Redd just lies there and waits to feel the heat of bullets piercing his flesh. Instead, he watches Rashan calmly put the gun back under his shirt.

"I did that so you would know, if I wanted you dead, you'd be dead. I had nothing to do with what happened to you today. I still think you a bitch, and you probably messing with that cop you always around, but I done known your punk-ass since middle school. My momma loves you, so I can't shoot you. Whoever it was, it wasn't me. I know you knew we were gonna get raided that night. You shoulda told me. You ever play me out like that again, my momma just gonna hafta be mad," Rashan says.

Redd nods his head in agreement with Rashan and they share a quick moment of mutual respect. He turns to leave, and Redd continues sipping his drink.

"Bastard," Redd says, under his breath. The door opens again and Redd's girlfriend rushes in. She hugs him and tries not to let him go. After telling her, he's fine, she tells him that he should tell her where all his finances can be accessed in case something like this happens in the future. Frustrated, he tells her he needs to get some rest so she would leave.

Redd sits up for the next couple of hours thinking about his life choices. He knows his girlfriend just wants his money, but he keeps her around anyway. He's done a lot of things that he's not proud of, but he's never come as close to death as he did earlier today. His love for money consumes him, and he's compromised his few remaining morals he had to get it.

Kora is driving through the city streets questioning her life choices. She feels like the world is against her, and she can't understand why at this point, it's still not a priority to anyone but her. The only constant she's had throughout her life is

Redd, and despite his questionable choices, today is the closest she's ever come to losing that.

The door to Redd's room opens and Kora walks in quietly, without turning on the light. She walks over and He begins to wake up slowly. Kora doesn't say anything: she just begins to undress. She stares at him while she does it, moving very slowly. The moonlight is coming in the window and bouncing off of Kora's slim but thick body. Redd watches her intently and is out of his hospital gown in two seconds flat. She climbs on top of him and slowly begins to kiss his chest. Redd is too cool to moan, so he massages her back and butt with his good hand to show his approval. Kora works her way down pleasuring Redd until she reaches his midpoint, ramping up her efforts with heavy strokes and throaty pulls. After trying to maintain his coolness under pressure, the moment claims him, as Redd lets out a loud moan. He admires Kora's fit body as she works meticulously on him, while he struggles to keep quiet. The low hum of the hospital bed rising can be heard as Redd holds the button to sit up. He grabs under Kora's arm with his good hand and pulls her to his face. She kisses him quickly as he continues lifting her with his powerful grasp until he's facing her mid-section. There's no subtlety as Redd plows his face in, licking, pulling, kissing and tasting. Kora yelps in approval as Redd can feel his face covered in a mix of sweat and juices. He's not going to stop until he knows he's done it, and he can feel the pressure of Kora tightening up slowly. It becomes more intense as her yelps and moans become more frequent. She desperately tries to maintain her balance as Redd continues to hold her up with one arm. Kora lets out a loud moan as she enjoys the effects of an extremely powerful climax. She makes her way down and kisses Redd as he accepts her.

"There's the breakthrough I needed," she whispers.

Her eyes widen as he reaches depths she didn't think were possible. Kora moves slowly up and down staring into Redd's face while he holds her as tightly as he can with one hand. She slowly grinds as Redd can feel his left side beginning to tingle. She leans back and begins to speed up, as the moonlight continues to shine on her flawless body. The visual is too much for Redd, as he continues to try to hold out. The movement, the body, the heat and the thrill, all take control of him. Redd climaxes, letting out a loud moan, and exhaling deeply.

"That was pretty fast," Kora says, while getting off the bed.

"Sorry, Special K. I had an intense day," Redd says.

"Yeah, we'll go with that," she says, getting dressed.

"You make me sick," he says playfully.

"I know I do. That's my job. I'm glad you're okay Redd," she tells him.

"Hey, me too. They wanted to keep me one night cause my blood pressure was high. I don't think this helped," he laughs.

"Redd, I'm being serious. You're the only reliable thing I've ever had in my life. I'm glad I didn't lose that. I'll see you when you get back home," she says, heading for the door.

As she walks out, Redd's roommate is laying under the cover with the pillow over his head. He's peeking out terrified. He can't believe what he just heard and partially saw.

CHAPTER TEN

Hurts A Little Bit

Google is sitting at his desk typing effortlessly while occasionally sipping on a Chai Tea. Kora walks up and gives him a fist bump. She goes into her office and sits down at her desk, putting her stuff down. Slumping down in her chair, she takes a deep breath before turning on her computer. She slowly looks through some of the open missing persons cases, and all the clues she's had.

"Long night Detective?" Asks Google, walking in.

"Unfortunately, not long enough," she says, shaking her head.

"I know the feeling," he says.

"I really don't think you do Google," she says with a light grin.

"Oh, wait, was that a reference to coitus? If so, then I don't know the feeling," he admits.

"Yes, I know. Let's move on. Are you having a productive morning?" she asks.

"I believe so. A young man named Bit called your desk phone about thirty minutes ago. He said he tried your cell last night. He claims he has some information you would find valuable," Google says.

"What exactly did he say?" Kora asks.

"Uh…*Yo, tell Merrit I know some shit, and she need to hit me up, you feel me?*" Google says, imitating him badly.

"That was much more offensive than I expected it to be. He's not answering. Get in the car, we'll stop by the park," she says.

When they arrive at the park, there's three police cruisers parked with their lights on. Officers are putting up tape. There are people crowding around being nosey. Kora and Google walk in and try to figure out what's going on. They flash their badges and walk under the tape. Google can feel the nervousness Kora is feeling. She sees a familiar face and tries to get answers.

"Officer Palmer? Curtis?" She calls out.

"What happened?" She asks.

"A shooting. Black male, 22 years old, was shot twice in the chest. His name was Courtney Flores. He went by the street name Bit. Apparently, he was sitting on that bench with some of his boys and a man just walked up and shot him. He took off running and the victim's friends all shot at him with unregistered firearms, so…they're going to jail. Kora looks over at Tito, Rowe, and Will in handcuffs and takes a deep breath. She can see the sadness in their faces, and as a cop, especially a woman, she knows she has to try and control the emotions she's feeling.

"Hey, I know you guys are pissed and hurt. I'll get you out of this: you have my word. Who did this? Was it a rival gang?" She asks.

"Naw, we was chillin', and this old head came in the park and shot Bit. He had to be almost forty," Tito says.

"He had some gray hairs in his beard. He had a cap and shades on. We couldn't get a good look," Rowe says.

"He had a tattoo on his hand. It was a Chinese letter or something. It looked stupid," Will says.

"Okay, I'll figure this out. I want yall to stay low and I'll get you out before you get to the county," Kora promises.

"Aight," they all say as they're led toward the squad cars.

"I guess you'll be giving the mayor a call," Google says.

"Yeah, I will. What the hell was Bit gonna tell me? Is that information what got him killed? Why didn't the killer shoot all of them?" She asks.

"He knew something that somebody didn't want anyone to know. Maybe we should question his family. I'll look him up," says Google.

"We're close. You know we're close," she says.

"How do you know?" He asks.

"They're killing people to keep information from us. Someone's gonna pay for that," she says.

"Why's that officer looking at you like that?" Asks Google.

"He likes me. He's okay, but cops aren't supposed to date cops. I…kind of deal with someone, though. He knows that. I thought about it: I mean, he is fine, but they would love to try to jam me up at the precinct," she says.

"I think I would've been fine if you would've just said *I don't know*," he says.

"Shut up Google," Kora says, walking toward the car.

Redd is released from the hospital and is happy to get in his truck and head home. His thoughts are all over the place, as he was sure that Rashan was the one who tried to take him out. Unsure if it's safe to go home, he decides to try anyway. He does his usual routine: stopping on Fourth Avenue to get his soul food before heading home. He thought about stopping at Walgreens to fill his prescription, but he just wants to get home and relax. When he finally pulls up, there's a police officer outside talking to Sascha's Mother and her boyfriend. She's in tears and looks frantic. He gets out the truck and hurries up to them to see what's going on. She tells him that unfortunately, Sascha didn't come home from school today. When she called the school, they told her that Sascha never made it to school. Her cell phone is off. The officer is unenthusiastically taking notes.

"Okay Ma'am, there's not much we can do until she's been missing for 48 hours. I'll follow up with you tomorrow to see if she's turned up. In the meantime, here's my card," the officer says, handing her a card and walking away.

"Redd, please help me get my baby back, please!" She begs, grabbing his shirt.

"Why you beggin' this dude? He aint nobody," Trevor says.

"I'll do whatever I can," Redd tells her.

"Thank you Redd! Thank you sooo much!" She tearfully said.

The next day Kora closes down Friday's with J.J. They filled up on appetizers and drinks. After a long embrace, they go their separate ways. Kora concentrated on enjoying JJ's company, instead of telling him about all the pressure she's under at work. After getting in the car, she thinks long and hard about whether or not she's ready to head to that lonely apartment. She pulls out of the driveway of Fridays and sees a bar across the street that looks like it's still open. She heads over and plops down on a stool right in front of the bartender. It's pretty empty, just a few scattered people.

"Hi Beautiful, what are you having?" He asks.

"You have Mountain Dew?" she asks with a half-smile.

"I sure do," he says, pouring it from the tap.

He slides the glass over to her and smiles. She lifts it and gives him a nod of approval. Kora feels like her brain has grown ten times bigger over the past few weeks, but it's still not enough to stop this madness. She keeps running through everything she knows so far, hoping she comes across something she's missing. Unfortunately, she keeps hitting the same dead end.

"You look like a woman with a lot on her mind," the bartender says.

"I do. Sometimes it feels like everyone is against me. I've always got a lot on my mind though," she says.

"Well, I hear that Hennessey can open up brain pathways and help with the thought process," he says.

"I've always been told it does the opposite. I'm not much of a drinker. For me, bars have my soda on tap, the best appetizers, and a good atmosphere to think," says Kora.

"Our wings are the best, trust me," he says.

"I just ate. I literally just came in here after eating,"

"Tell you what: I'm gonna bring you six wings on the house. If you like them, when you like them, you have to promise to come back and eat," he says.

"I can't say no to free stuff," she laughs.
"Good. They call me Doc,"

"I'm Kora," she says.

"I'll be right back: I have to go to the bathroom. Wait, why do they call you Doc?" She asks.

"Back in 85, I did a year of medical school. It didn't work out, but the name stuck. Hey, I can still stitch you up if you need stitches though," he says.

"That's good to know," Kora says, standing up and walking to the back.

She makes her way past a couple of booths and tables in the back of the bar. Although she's in a hurry to pee, she sees a familiar face. Once she reaches the bathroom, she thinks for a minute:

"Was that Captain Rainer? I didn't think he was a drinker," she thinks to herself.

As much as she can't stand him, she knows it would be considered disrespectful to see your captain somewhere and not acknowledge him. The thought of having to speak to him turns her stomach. In this world that she lives in, he can get away with saying the disrespectful things to her that he says all the time, yet if she gives the slightest pushback, it's considered insubordination. She looks in the mirror at her tired eyes and tries to put a little water on them. She walks back out and sees that it is indeed the captain. He's sitting at a booth with another guy. She walks up and sees a surprised look on the captain's face.

"Merrit? What are you doing here?" He asks.

"Oh, just having some wings," she says.

"I see. Well, I would tell you it's late to be out on a work night, but I have to go in tomorrow as well, so carry on. You better be on time tomorrow though," he says.

As Kora turns to walk away, she takes a quick look at the man sitting with Captain Rainer. He's a light skinned man with glasses on. She glances at his hand and sees a Chinese letter tattooed on it! She does a double take and then quickly walks off. She tells Doc to bag the wings so she can head out. She wants to sneak and take a picture, but the captain and the man are both looking at her.

"Do me favor Doc: see those two guys sitting at that booth in the back? If you can, get a quick picture of the light skinned one when you get a chance," she says in a loud whisper, while dropping her card on the bar and quickly flashing her badge.

"No problem officer. I'll text it to your number," he says, looking at her card.

"Thanks Doc. Have a good night," she says.

Kora quickly gets in her car pulls off. Her mind is flooded with thoughts. Was that the guy that killed Bit? Does the Captain know he's a criminal? Was it just coincidence? She wants to wake up Google, but she knows it's too late. Maybe some sleep is what she needs to reset and refocus. She drives home struggling to focus on the road. She's been going so hard that she hasn't had decent rest in a while. It's almost 3:30am, so tonight won't be any different. When she gets home, Kora doesn't even undress. She kicks her shoes off and gets in the bed. She's asleep within five minutes.

When Google walks into work the next morning, he can feel something is off. As he walks down the hallway, he notices a few of the officers staring at him on the low.

The energy in the building feels unusual. He sits at his desk and looks around, trying to figure out why. He powers on his computer and looks over his shoulder. Some of the officers are looking at him but turn away when he turns toward them. He goes back to typing, wondering if he just woke up on the wrong side of the bed this morning. He goes through the morning reports and highlights anything that could be helpful to Kora. After about thirty minutes, she comes walking in. There's bags under her eyes, and she's moving slowly towards her office. Google puts out his fist for a bump, but she completely ignores it. Kora opens her office door and drops her bag on the floor. She slumps down at her desk and puts her head down. Within ten seconds, she's lightly snoring.

Google walks in and sees her sleeping at her desk. He closes the door and her window shades.

"Detective?" He whispers.

"Go away Google," she said, half asleep.

"Listen, you need to wake up. I saw something in the daily reports from yesterday that you might find interesting," he prompted.

"I'm sure it's another dead-end Google. Everything always leads to a dead end. You know the boys in the park said that the shooter was a guy with a Chinese letter or symbol tattooed on his hand? Last night, I saw Captain Rainer in a bar having a drink with a guy that had a Chinese letter or symbol tattooed on his hand. I got excited for minute, but I know it won't lead to anything," she says.

"Did the symbol look like this?" Google asked, drawing a Chinese letter on her notepad.

"Yeah it did. How do you know that?" She asked.

"That guy comes to visit the captain sometimes. His name is Stewart Funchess. He works for the Coast Guard. They served together in the Persian Gulf War," says Google.

"What did you look him up before?" She asked.

"Actually, that information is a result of my occasional eavesdropping," he admitted.

"That's honest of you. What was in the morning report?" She asked.

"A woman by the name of Zakiyyah Hawes has a young daughter, Sascha, who never came home from school the other day. When she called the school, they told her that her daughter never showed up that day. The interesting part is that Sascha got back home last night," he said, looking at the report.

"I know that name. Sascha Hawes. Wait a minute, does she live on Arlington Avenue?" She asks.

"Yes, she does," said Google.

"That's the girl that Redd spends time with," Kora says, grabbing her keys and heading for the door.

Google follows behind her with all the ruffled papers, trying not to drop any.

"I don't understand. Who's Redd?" He asked.

"A friend of mine. He looks after her like she's his daughter. I wonder if he knew she was missing. You said she turned up back home?" Asked Kora.

"Yes. There's no details in this report on what exactly happened though," he said rifling through the papers.

Redd was on his way home from work. He was blasting his music and smoking weed. It's been a long night, and he's exhausted. The Port was busy all night. His phone rang, and he saw that it was his girlfriend. He'd been trying to break up with her for a while. Redd reluctantly agreed to stop by her house on his way home. Even though he wanted to go home and get some sleep, now was as good a time as any to get it over with. He turns around and quickly turns his music down as he sees a cop parked on the corner. His phone rings again, and he quickly answers it:

"When? Yeah. I'll be there on time. Aight," he says.

Kora and Google pull up to the home of Zakiyyah Hawes. She rents the bottom floor of a small three-bedroom house on Arlington Avenue. It's a familiar area for Kora, as the home sits right next door to Redd's apartment. She has seen and spoken to Sascha on multiple occasions at Redd's place.

"Let me do the talking Google. You scare people when you speak," Kora says.

"I wasn't aware of that," he smiles.

They ring the doorbell and Zakiyyah opens the door after a short wait.

"Hi, I'm Detective Merrit, he's Detective Sitmore. We have some questions regarding your daughter's abduction. May we come in?" Kora asks.

"Sure," she says, opening the door.

"Ms. Kora!" Sascha said running up to her.

She gave her a big hug and didn't let go. Google smiled uncomfortably and made his way over to the couch. Sascha finally let Kora go and sat on the couch next to Google. She was intrigued by how short he was

"Are you a man or a boy?" She asked him confused.

"I guess that depends on who you ask," he responded embarrassed.

Kora was trying her hardest not to laugh, but it wasn't easy.

"What are you doing here Ms. Kora? Ms. Kora is Redd's friend," Sascha said.

"Oh," Zakiyyah said with hate in her eyes.

"We just wanted to follow up. We know that Sascha was abducted. Can you tell us what happened?" Kora asked.

"When she didn't come home from school I called: they told me she never made it to school that day. I drove around and searched everywhere. I called the police and they said there was nothing they could do until she was missing for 48 hours. I was pissed off. I asked anyone in the neighborhood that was willing to help to search," Zakiyyah stated.

"How did you get her back?" Asked Kora.

The doorbell rang. I ran to it, and there was Redd standing there holding Sascha's hand. He found her! I haven't let her out my sight since," Zakiyyah replied.

"Do you mind if I ask Sascha about it?" Kora asked.

"No, that's fine," Zakiyyah agreed.

"Sascha, what happened to you that day?" Kora asked.

"I was walking to school and a white van came and the man asked me if I knew where Shoprite was. I was telling him and then a whole bunch of men jumped out of the van and grabbed me," Sascha s said.

"Where did they take you?" Kora questions.

"I don't know. I was in the van and it was dark. Then I was in a building. They never turned the lights on. There was a loud bell! I heard men arguing. Oh, I heard horns! I fell asleep, and I woke up in Redd's car and he was driving me home," she says.

"He's my guardian angel. I owe him everything," Zakiyyah said, putting her hand on her chest.

"Do you remember anything else?" Kora asked Sascha, cutting an annoyed look at Zakiyyah.

"They kept saying Friday. Don't mess up Friday," Sascha said.

Kora had a blank expression on her face. She's drifted off and is deep in thought. The voices of Google and Zakiyyah sound like distant dream sounds as everything is being tuned out. Kora's eyes are closed as she is focused on everything she's heard recently. Google looks at her confused, as everyone seems to be waiting for her to talk.

"So uh, Sascha, did they say anything else? Do you know what they meant by Friday? Do you think that was a code for something?" Google asked, trying to get the spotlight off of his partner.

"I don't remember anything else. Wait, they kept saying 1300. I remember because I want to be thirteen really bad," she said.

"You will one day Sweetie. Trust me, you don't want to rush that. Thank you both for your time. We'll let you get back to it," Kora said, signaling Google.

"Are you going to tell me what's going on?" Google asked as they get back in the car.

"It's bad. I think I understand why we're hitting all these dead ends. I-I just need a minute to think," she says.

"Okay, go ahead. I'm here if you need me," Google stated.

"I'm gonna need you. If I'm right, we got a big problem," she said.

CHAPTER ELEVEN

Like Father, Like Daughter

When they arrived at the police station, Captain Rainer was standing outside. He watched their car pull up and didn't take his eyes off them.

"Uh, are we in trouble?" Google whispered as Kora puts the car in park.

"We're gonna be in a lot of trouble, sir," she said, opening her car door.

"Merrit, can I have a word please?" Captain Rainer inquired.

"I'll start writing the Hawes report. I'll see you inside," Google said, walking past the captain and into the precinct.

"What can I do for you captain?" She asked.

"I think it's time I took you off the missing people's cases," he informed her.

"Is that right? Why is that sir?" She asked.

"Save it. I don't know what you think you're doing, but it ends now," the captain said with concern in his voice.

"I see. Am I getting too close?" She asked

"What are you talking about?" The captain asked

"I believed all that talk you gave me about going through the ranks the right way. You left some stuff out though," she stated.

"You better choose the next thing you say very carefully," the captain warned.

"I know what you really are," Kora said with a slight grin and raised eyebrow.

"Yes, I'm your superior. I know you think you run this place, but you don't," he said.

"Everyone that has a hand in the abductions of these girls is going down," she promised.

"Is that right? I hope so," he smirked.

"You're not taking me off these cases. Don't make me call the mayor," she threatened.

"That's right, your friend the mayor. You think these abductions are connected, correct?" he asked.

"You know they are!"

"If they are, Detective, a lot of people would stand to lose a lot of money if that operation was stopped," he said with a slick grin.

"I hope so. That *'operation'* is about to be stopped. Everyone that has a hand in it in any way is going down," Kora promised.

"That might be a lot of people Detective: a lot of your people. If your blood doesn't bleed blue, you're in the wrong place," he said.

"My blood bleeds red: like all the sistas that have disappeared on your watch. You're the worst kind of bastard. I knew you weren't a real black man from the start: no facial hair, driving a 3 series, pronouncing the whole *i-n-g* on the end of all your words. You're a sellout, and I'm gonna bury you…John Doe," Kora said.

"Well, you better dig a hole big enough for a whole lot of folks," he said, giving her a look and walking off.

Kora watched him walk away angrily. She tried to call Redd, but he didn't answer. Now that she had figured out what's going on, she knew that was only half the battle. She had to formulate a plan and do it quick. She took a moment and thought about her father, and all the cases he'd closed. She also thought back on the case he didn't solve. Reluctantly she went inside and told Google she was going home to get some rest: letting him know she's going to pick him up at midnight. With so much on her mind, she had to focus. As soon as Kora got home, she set her alarm and went to bed.

Kora is driving across town to Googles Place. She's focused, but a little nervous. The quiet streets in the city almost feel deserted. Even though she was born in New York, Kora loves the city of East Orange. She's a fixture everywhere. She gets her hair done on Main Street, gets her food from the local restaurants, and is known to jog around the city. Sometimes she wonders if she never knew about the abductions, how different would her life be? Since taking down the casket boys, it's been a whirlwind. Her phone begins to ring, but she doesn't recognize the number. She stares at it on the screen until the voicemail picks it up. As she turns the corner to Googles place, the phone rings again with the unknown number.

"This is Merrit," she replied.

"Hello Daughter. How are you?" Maya responded.

"What the hell do you want?" Kora huffed.

"Are you okay? I'm just checking on you," her mother said.

"You're not just checking on me. What do you want?"

"I want you to come and see me again. There's so much we should talk about," Maya finally stated.

"You want to talk? You want to talk about how you lured my father to his death? How about all the people you killed? All the families you destroyed. How much sadness you and your crew caused? What exactly do we need to talk about?" Kora quizzed.

"I'm not perfect okay. I've made a lot of mistakes. I'm paying for them."

"A mistake is something you didn't mean to do. Every life you took, every execution you and your crew took part in, you did on purpose. The only mistake you made was you got caught."

"That's fair. If you ever let me help you, you know I will," Maya conceded.

"I'll keep that in mind," she responded unenthusiastically.'

"I'll leave you with this: one thing I'll give your dad, he never trusted anybody, and he never went into anything without a solid plan, and a backup plan."

"I'll keep that in mind," Kora said without emotion.

"I hope you do. Come and see me tomorrow," Maya requested

"Don't hold your breath," she says, disconnecting the call.

Kora thinks for a minute, reflecting on their brief conversation while she texts Google to come outside. She reluctantly dials a number.

"I-I need a favor. You have to do it my way though. When I say my way, you have to do exactly what I say. I'm gonna send you a text. What? Come on! Why do I have to say that? You're such an asshole. Fine, I'll say it," she says.

Port Newark, a major component of the Port of New York and New Jersey, is the principal container ship facility for goods entering and leaving the New York metropolitan area. Located on Newark Bay, it's run by the Port Authority.

Most nights, it's busy with longshoreman, shipments coming in and out, and loud noise. The third Friday of every month however, there's no activities scheduled at the Port. Officially, no business happens at the Port on this night: unofficially, it's the most lucrative evening every month. This is the night that doesn't officially exist at the port.

Redd is standing at the edge of the water holding a clipboard. A white van pulls up close to him. Two men get out and walk around back to open the doors. They shake hands with Redd first. Kora is watching with Google from a distance with binoculars. When the doors open and Kora sees the chained-up girls in the back, her heart sinks. She drops the binoculars and stares off into space. The frown on her face clearly displays her disappointment. She shook off the hurt and told Google they were heading down there.

"Kora," he said looking through the binoculars.

"Those two guys that were in the van are both cops from our precinct," he continued.

"Yeah I know, come on," she ordered.

They unloaded six women from the van and Redd was filling out their information on his clipboard. They were crying and struggling to get free, with no luck. The large white boat that was docked in front of Redd had one light shining onto the dock. There were two men standing at the front of the pier by the boat. They were both armed. The two men from the van pushed the women to the ground.

"Any trouble?" Redd asked.

"Naw, no trouble. We should've had ten though. You got em checked in?" One of the men asked.

"Yeah, take em on board," Redd ordered.

"Nobody move!" Kora yelled, coming out from behind a wall with Google.

Everyone looks at her stunned, while Redd stares at her disappointed and shocked. The men from the van and the boat all pull their guns and point them at Her and Google. Redd drops the clipboard and can't take his eyes off her.

"Kora, what the hell!?! What are you doing here?!" Redd yelled, pulling his gun.

"You're all under arrest: all of you! Redd, you're a sorry bastard. It's like you said: nothing happens at the port, without you knowing about it. You shouldn't have rescued her. When you got Sascha back: that's when I knew. Women have been disappearing forever, and you managed to get her back to her mother within twenty-four hours. The only way you coulda done that is if you knew about what was going on. I looked the other way Redd. I looked the other way while you dealt drugs, stole, and did a whole lotta dirty shit. I thought you had morals though. I never thought you were capable of this. Get on the ground!" She demanded.

"I'm sorry, Special K. I can't do that though," Redd said.

She heard several guns clicking behind her and Google. Kora turned around slowly to see six familiar faces holding guns. They're all police from her own precinct: including her former partner Mills!

"I told you before, rook, you can't change the world. I'm gonna enjoy this," Mills taunted.

"So, this is why it was such a struggle to find out what was happening to these girls. You're all involved. You're all getting rich off the backs of these poor girls. You tried to stop us at every turn, and you failed," Kora challenged.

"Failed? You're about to die Merrit," a familiar voice said from over her shoulder.

She turned around again slowly to see Captain Rainer standing with Officer Palmer and the man with the tattooed hand. They all had their guns pointed at Kora and Google also.

"I never liked you. Women are too goddamned hardheaded. You all don't listen to shit. You were a pain in the ass from day one. A typical broad, thinking you're entitled to preferential treatment. Palmer here was supposed to get close to you, but you're such a bitch, he couldn't. You should've just minded your business. I'm not John Doe, this gentleman next to me is," said the captain, lightly pointing at the man with the tattooed hand.

"Years ago, when we brought him in for kidnapping and sex trafficking, he told us how much he was making, and how much we could all make if he had us on board. The rest is history,"

"You're a disgrace: you all are. You've been at this for years, taking young black women for what, money? And you call yourself a captain, a black one at that, and you're pimpin sistas out with these white boys?" Kora asked.

"You should stop talking, Kora. I can't help you anymore. I love you, you know that, but my money comes first," Redd said.

"Save it, Redd. You're such a dumbass, you don't even realize these idiots you're working with are the ones that tried to kill you," she informed him.

"What are you talking about?" He asked.

"You're the only one here without a badge idiot. How long do you think they were gonna keep you around? This is an operation to kidnap women and ship them overseas. People are getting rich. The people involved have badges: you don't. They tried once: tonight was gonna be your last night," she said.

"What's she talking about? Is that true?" Redd asked everyone.

"Why are you listening to her? You know you're one of us. She's about to die, she's gonna say anything to save her skin. It's too late though," The captain growled.

Redd still looked confused as he stood with his clipboard trying to analyze what Kora said.

"How long have you been involved Redd? They needed a longshoreman so they could know the schedule at night. They paid you and you went right along with it. They know the schedule now. What did you think was gonna happen?" Kora asked.

"Is that true man? Is anything she saying true?" Redd inquired.

"Redd, you gotta relax. Think about how much money you've made. How much we all have made. Get those bitches on the boat. They got a long ride," the captain tried to reason with him.

"You're not even a man," Kora told Redd.

"Come on. I gotta look out for myself. I need this extra loot. Who's gonna look out for me?" Redd asked.

"Who looked out for those missing girls Redd? Who looks out for them?" Kora asked.

"Okay, enough talk. Somebody put a bullet in their heads so we can get on with our business," John Doe said.

"Hold up, do we gotta kill her though? I'm sayin', let me just holla at her for a minute. Maybe we can work this out," Redd pleaded.

"Redd, get the women on the boat and mind your business," The captain ordered, pointing his gun at him.

"Merrit, I thought about just putting a bullet in your head myself, but there's a lot of boys on the force that want to enjoy that moment also: in particular your old partner. I'm thinking a firing squad may be more appropriate for this situation. Boys, let's all light her up, and her annoying ass partner. Is there any militant, smart ass words you'd like to say before we Swiss cheese you both?" The captain asks, grinning.

"Unfortunately, yes," she said, taking a deep, disappointed sigh.

"Agent Austin is the finest black man in the entire bureau," she continued, rolling her eyes.

"Huh," everyone said confused, looking around.

"Everyone on the pier, this is Agent Austin of the F.B.I. You are completely surrounded. Put your weapons down and get on the ground immediately. We will shoot anyone that moves from this point on," an amplified voice said.

Bright spotlights hit every spot of the pier, making it look as if it's daytime. F.B.I. agents are everywhere. The dirty cops know they're surrounded, and the only way off the pier is either in the water or past all of the agents. John Doe looks around and panics. He takes a step toward the boat and is immediately shot. He falls forward and his lifeless body is crumpled up for everyone to see.

"Would anyone else like to try us?" Austin asked.

"I'm not going to jail. I hate you Merrit! I hate you!" Mills yelled, raising his gun at her.

Mills is shot and hits the ground. He writhed in pain and Kora shook her head.

"Still a jackass," she said.

"Put your weapons down now!" Austin demands.

One by one, they all placed their weapons down on the pier. They laid on their stomachs and waited to be arrested. Redd didn't move though. He looked at everyone laying down and the realization of what was happening sank in.

"Redd, put your gun down and get on the ground," Kora ordered

"I can't, Special K. I can't go to jail. I'll be in there the rest of my life," he said.

"You'll get a lawyer. These cops coerced you. You had to go along, or they would have killed you. Hell, they tried to kill you. I will help you Redd, I promise, but you have to put that gun down," she pleaded.

"When you took down the Casket Boys, that was your moment. You did your thing, and you been that chick ever since. This is my moment Kora. If I raise this gun, everyone's gonna talk about how I was that dude to the end," Redd said.

"Don't do that. They will kill you, Redd. I know you don't want to die on this pier. I'm mad as hell at you. I think you're a piece of shit right now. I know that bothers you. You want to change my mind? Drop the gun, get on the ground, and cooperate. Tell us where these women are being sent. Tell us who the people are on the other side waiting for these *shipments*. If you do that, you have a chance Redd. Don't die without trying to make it right. You were my hero growing up. I looked up to you. You had my back through everything. We were in those shitty group homes together. If they shoot you, people aren't gonna say you were that dude to the end. They're gonna say he sold his people out and was helping smuggle abducted young black girls out of the country. He was shot like a dog on a pier. Is that what you want? If it is, then raise that gun and be that dude," she said.

Redd looked around and saw dozens of F.B.I. Agents on the pier with their guns all drawn. The bright lights had him straining his eyes. He was holding his gun in his hand, trying to figure out what to do. Kora watched him intensely, waiting to see what happened.

"I'm sorry Kora. I ain't no snitch either. I get it, but I can't. Redd Duncan ain't gonna be no informant. Tell everybody, Redd wasn't scared of …"

A shot rang out from Kora's left side. It hits Redd in the leg, and he falls. The gun lands too far away from him, as he grabs his leg in pain. She looks over and sees Google with a smoking gun.

"Statistically speaking, if he didn't put his gun down after your passionate plea, more than likely he was going to raise his gun and accept the final outcome," Google recited.

"Good job, Google," Kora commended.

"Really?" He asked.

"Yeah. I think you just saved Redd's life," she informed him.

The F.B.I. went around and arrested everyone, picking up weapons and tagging everything. They seized the boat and found two more women inside of it. There was a ledger on the boat with dates and locations. An agent handed the ledger to Austin, who looked at it and smiled.

"This is the type of bust that makes a career Kora. You just exposed a network of dirty cops. I'm guessing there's no law enforcement job in the country you couldn't have right now," Austin stated.

"I don't care about that. Where were these girls headed?" Kora asked.

"Looks like Cuba. If I'm reading this right," he said.

"We'll reach out to the Cuban authorities in the morning," Austin promised.

"Good. You will keep me posted on how that goes, right?"

"Of course. And if you change your mind and decide to see what this meal called dinner is all about, you'll call me right?" He asked.

"You have no shot, Austin. But don't stop asking me," she responded with a slick grin.

The Mayor of East Orange gets out of his car and walks up to her along with the Kurt Vino, the Chief of Police. Mayor Brown stops Kora before she can say a single slick word and hugs her tightly. She's a little confused but she goes with it and looks at the giant Kool Aid smile on Kurt's face while the long embrace happens.

"Ummm.... okay.... it's my friend, Mayor Brown that always gives me a hard time, and now he's a big old hugging machine," she teased.

"Three years ago, I got an anonymous call. They told me to not to probe all the abductions of young black women in my city. I ignored them and even tried to step up the investigations. Two months later, my daughter disappeared without a trace. We never heard anything: no ransom, no calls, nothing. We gave up on ever finding Hazel. It may not happen, but you've given my family hope. I owe you so much. You know you're getting a key to the city for this," he said.

"Well deserved Detective. You exposed a network of dirty cops in our department and I'm proud of you. I know all the forces you fought through to make this happen. You're the best of all of us. It goes without saying, but you can have any job in this city you want, except mine. And hell, that's probably negotiable at this point. You come and see me when you're ready, so I can beg you to take the new captain's position that's been opened thanks to that dirty bastard, Captain Rainer," Kurt said, extending his hand.

"I appreciate that Chief. See that little guy over there?" She said, shaking his hand and pointing to Google.

"Yeah?" The Chief questioned.

"That's Detective Spencer Sitmore. We call him Google. He's a great partner. He's a genius and he's been instrumental in helping me take down this operation," Kora stated.

"Is that right? Thank you for telling me that. I'll be meeting with him also. I'm coordinating with the PNR in the morning. They should hopefully be able to assist with tracking down some of the missing. PNR is…"

"Policia Nacional Revoluncionaria. They're under the administration of the Cuban Ministry of the Interior. That damn Google is rubbing off on me," laughed Kora.

"That's impressive. I don't know what's next for you, but we're damn proud," Kurt says.

He and the Mayor walked away from her and over to the news cameras. Kora soaked in all that has happened while staring into the night sky. She watched as paramedics tended to Redd's leg while he struggled with handcuffs on. She turned to see Captain Rainer and Officer Mills loaded into an FBI armored vehicle. As much as Kora wanted to enjoy the moment, it didn't feel like a victory to her. All those missing women were still just that: missing. She took out her dad's badge and looked at it for a few moments. Kora felt a tear well up in the corner of her eye, but quickly wiped it away to maintain her toughness.

"There's nothing wrong with showing emotion," Google said, walking up to her.

"I know that. I guess I just don't know how to feel right now."

"Well, your father solved 1,536 cases. It wasn't until year five that he solved his first major case. You've already surpassed him in a way," Google stated.

"I would ask you how you know that, but there would be no point in that," Kora said.

"I appreciate what you told the Chief. You didn't have to do that," he replied.

"You're good people Google. I'm glad you're my partner. I hope whatever happens, we stay partners," she told him.

"I would like that," he responded.

"Google, I'm going to get a burger. I know it's past your bedtime, but do you want to go?" Kora quizzed.

"Absolutely," he said.

As they begin to walk to the car, Austin holds up his hand to get her attention. He puts his phone down and tells her he has some news. Koa looks at him confused and feels a rush of sadness. His eyes are telling the story before he even opens his mouth.

Two hours ago

At the black site prison that doesn't officially exist, dinner had just ended, and the inmates were in their cells for the night. It was quiet in the dimly lit hallways. At the beginning of the cell block, a corrections officer is sitting at the desk reading a book. He's fighting to stay awake. While reaching for a five-hour energy, a small needle hits neck. The officer's face hits the desk as he's out cold. A few minutes later, another corrections officer is checking the cells, making sure the inmates are all accounted for. The giant man makes his way down the dark winding hallway. He noticed the guard face down at the desk and smiled, thinking he was sleeping. He walked over to him and playfully slapped him on the back of his head. When there was no movement, his smile quickly faded, and he tried to wake him up. Before the officer could pick up the phone, a small needle hits his neck, sending him crashing to the floor.

Maya was sitting on her bed playing solitaire. Her cell has pictures of beaches all over the walls. There's a small television that she never turns on. The sound of a key card at her cell door makes Maya turn around. Three corrections officers come into her cell, Maya smiles. They remove their hats and it's her old crew: Tess, Angie, and Cian. They look at her with disappointed faces. Cian begins screwing a silencer on the end of a handgun.

"Maya, just hang yourself. Don't make us shoot you," Tess said.

"I went around the world with you ladies. We killed so many people. It was fun, I can't even lie. I got busted, and you left me in here for over two decades. You never tried to get me out, never reached out to me, nothing. Now, after all this time, you show up to kill me," Maya laughs.

"We don't have a choice Maya," Cian said.

"I know. You saw that my daughter found me. You can't take the risk of me telling her anything. I knew you'd come. I got news for ya'll though: she's good. She's really good. She'll come for you. He had a heart: that's why we beat him. She doesn't have one," Maya grinned.

"We'll have to kill her Maya. We'll have to kill your daughter," Angie promises.

"Good luck with that. She's different," Maya says, closing her eyes.

At the Port

Austin explained to Kora what happened at the jail while they were at the port. He's standing with Google. Kora is standing at the edge of the port looking out at the water. She has tears in her eyes. Having finally found her mother, it's a lot for her to have lost her that fast. Kora is also aware that she's the reason the remaining ghost members came back and killed Maya. Ten minutes pass as she stares at the water, wondering if she should have been more receptive to her mother. After wiping her face, she walks back over to Google and Austin.

"I'm gonna catch those bitches once and for all. They're mine," Kora says with tears in her eyes.

www.ingramcontent.com/pod-product-compliance
Lightning Source LLC
LaVergne TN
LVHW020713110826
845149LV00012B/2239

* 9 7 8 0 9 8 9 8 6 4 2 1 3 *